HARD OL' SPOT

AN ANTHOLOGY OF
ATLANTIC CANADIAN FICTION

© 2009, Mike Heffernan

We gratefully acknowledge the financial support of the Canada Council for the Arts, the Government of Canada through the Book Publishing Industry Development Program (BPIDP), and the Government of Newfoundland and Labrador through the Department of Tourism, Culture and Recreation for our publishing program.

All rights reserved. No part of this work covered by the copyrights hereon may be reproduced or used in any form or by any means—graphic, electronic or mechanical—without the prior written permission of the publisher. Any requests for photocopying, recording, taping or information storage and retrieval systems of any part of this book shall be directed in writing to the Canadian Reprography Collective, One Yonge Street, Suite 1900, Toronto, Ontario M5E 1E5.

Cover Design by Darren Whalen
Layout by Joanne Snook-Hann
Printed on acid-free paper

Published by
KILLICK PRESS
an imprint of CREATIVE BOOK PUBLISHING
a Transcontinental Inc. associated company
P.O. Box 8660, Stn. A
St. John's, Newfoundland and Labrador A1B 3T7

Printed in Canada by:
TRANSCONTINENTAL INC.

Library and Archives Canada Cataloguing in Publication

Hard ol' spot : an anthology of dark Atlantic Canadian fiction / edited by Mike Heffernan ; illustrated by Darren Whalen.

ISBN 978-1-897174-48-7

1. Short stories, Canadian (English)--Atlantic Provinces. 2. Canadian fiction (English)--21st century. I. Heffernan, Mike, 1978- II. Whalen, Darren
III. Title: Hard old spot.

PS8329.5.A85H37 2009   C813'.01089715
C2009-903836-6

HARD OL' SPOT

AN ANTHOLOGY OF ATLANTIC CANADIAN FICTION

SELECTED BY MIKE HEFFERNAN
ILLUSTRATED BY DARREN WHALEN

St. John's, Newfoundland and Labrador
2009

To those who came before us.

"Canadian writers as a whole do not trust Nature, because they are always suspecting some dirty trick."
– Margaret Atwood, *Survival*

"my outport

        suffers from the wounds

                of empty bones

        old houses

        where the field mice scatter holes

        about decay."

– Paul O'Neil, *Lost Outport*

"It was not that the breaking mirror brought them bad luck. Helen didn't believe that. But all the bad luck to come was in Cal's glance, and when he looked at the mirror the bad luck busted out."
– Lisa Moore, *February*

TABLE OF CONTENTS

THE BRIGHTEST SLIVER OF REDEMPTION:		
AN INTRODUCTION TO *HARD OL' SPOT*	Kathleen Winter	VII
BREAK, BREAK, BREAK	Gerard Collins	1
DRIVE-THRU	Elizabeth Blanchard	13
THE CHAIN AROUND MY NECK	Leslie Vryenhoek	23
EMINENT DOMAIN	Michelle Butler Hallett	37
A HOLE FULL OF NOTHING	Steve Vernon	45
NIGHT DIVIDES THE DAY	Lee D. Thompson	67
HOMECOMING	Keith Collier	75
SKY	Joanne Soper-Cook	91
HOLD OUT	Gerard Collins	101
THE NIGHT WATCHMAN	Michael Crummey	115
HER ADOLESCENCE	Sara Tilley	127
AT SEA	Don Roy	141
EVERYTHING WAS LOST IN THE FIRE	Craig Francis Power	147
AN APOLOGY	Ramona Dearing	153
ABOUT THE AUTHORS		169
ABOUT THE EDITOR		173
ABOUT THE ILLUSTRATOR		173
ACKNOWLEDGEMENTS		174

THE BRIGHTEST SLIVER OF REDEMPTION: AN INTRODUCTION TO *HARD OL' SPOT*

By Kathleen Winter

Who is in these stories, standing in the dark? Who is that bystander, that hardened observer, that watcher of lost dreams. What is this place where the wind takes anything it can find; where wind can make every nail in the clapboard of a house groan, and can rip the door of the family Chevette off its hinges? The ocean will swallow someone or something tonight, and other predators of the human soul roam the town.

If reading is a kind of dialogue, the act of writing is an earlier, more primitive form of conversation, between the writer and forces s/he does not necessarily understand at first. A writer, especially one confronted with dark material, asks conscious and unconscious questions as part of the act of getting the story down. The material might answer the writer in a civilized way, or it might continue to pile mystery, cloud and shadow. This makes things more fun for the writer, or more frightening, depending on the mischief of the material and on the artist's disposition.

The first question a writer might ask darkness is, "Where do you come from?" Location is everything, and, like light, darkness has many birthplaces. Does it come from social constructs: wartime; a dying pulp mill; a pit where the fist meets blood; a suburb where rape is a girl's first romance? Does darkness spill inside the person: is it a stifled longing for beauty; a lost softness; a personal sorrow turned to bitterness? Or is darkness born inside and out, in the heart of an immigrant stranger new in a lonesome town?

The second question a writer asks darkness is, "How long do you endure?" This question is central in an Atlantic Canadian fiction anthology. The words *Atlantic* and *relentless* are sisters; they sound the same. In them there is no slackening, no growing gentle, nor forgiving, nor growing softer. "How long do you go on?" asks the writer of his or her dark material. "Is there redemption? Can I give my reader one small slice of hope? Is there a transformation that will let my reader stop holding her breath? Can we live after this story, or will it always champion a kind of death? How cold are those rocks out on that beach anyway?" The writer asks these things because, though s/he wants to control the material, conditions are unpredictable: the material cuts the template and creates the rules. Creativity comes after chaos, not the other way around.

Craft is important, and so is art, and so is choosing the right word or cutting the wrong one. In many anthologies defined by place, the writer's job is to allow the power of place to come out adequately. In this Atlantic Canadian collection, the place does not ask for permission but instead exerts a power that the best writers have no choice but to restrain into a form of pressurized story trying to beat its way out from between the covers.

In *Break, Break, Break* by Gerard Collins, this pressure is elemental; it comes from rain leaking into a five-gallon bucket in the kitchen, from wind so brutal the narrator is afraid it will blow the house apart and leave her kneeling by the sink with her mother and brother, praying for the *Ocean Ranger*. It comes from restless country music in a tiny bungalow where a daughter thinks about the meaning of the word *forsaken* before the *Ocean Ranger* falls. Pressure here comes from the outside, demonic and awry.

Tension is more human in Steve Vernon's *A Hole Full of Nothing*, a story about a young man's longing for greatness that turns in on itself for want of an outlet. The anthology gets its title from the narrator's dad, complaining as he checks his scratch-and-win tickets after the death of the fishery; "A man can't even afford himself a decent drink these days... Nothing but lukewarm piss-thin tea, day after goddamn day, you talk about living shit-poor in a damn hard old spot." While the father is bereft, the real darkness here belongs to the son, whose yearning for glory turns a young man's prank to the sinister, violent spectacle on which Vernon's story turns.

While a hard place breeds violence, drunkenness and reckless escape, the writers in this collection draw on visionary elements as well. *Night Divides the Day* by Lee D. Thompson is a love story powered by yearning of one lover for the undefined and unattainable loveliness he senses in another. Jade is the girl Derek McDonald links with stars, with being airborne, with being the girl whom, in school, was "almost never there". The visionary and the intangible almost triumph on their own here, via stars, guitar music and youthful longing. There is a hallucinatory edge to the night; crystal meth, molly, coke, acid; and Thompson writes the cocktail with lethal and beautiful precision:

"We wrestled in the field. Her dark hair was like a nest. Tiny, she was curled in it, crying.

I was standing in the field for hours, swaying with the wind. The sun is a cathedral, I thought. You can hear it. I have to tell Jade the sun is a cathedral."

Thompson's story is one that moves the anthology from exterior motivation: wind hurling itself at you until you perish; water dashing us against stones: towards an inner voice and an interior story that happen in the realm of character, as psychic journey. Things happen not so much *to* a character as *within* him or her. Ramona Dearing's story, *An Apology*, a triumph of point of view, takes us further into the parts of this anthology that deal with who we are inside. Structure becomes increasingly important in stories that deal with the inner self, since memory is not linear, and a character's inner voice does not follow what we like to think of as ordinary time, orderly and consecutive. Gerard Lundrigan, accused of sexual abuse of orphans, thinks about his new puppy as he faces the jury. Through the relentless darkness of this story, Dearing lifts the material, energizes it with fresh points of view, with observations, startling juxtaposition, and inner voices of people who face each other from opposing angles and corners of the narrative. Like other writers, she also uses the wind. Though relentless, the story has vents. It does not moralize, and though it is at heart a story about judgment, it does not itself judge. "At first," Gerard Lundrigan remembers about his work with orphans, "God is everywhere."

Even more character-driven is Leslie Vryenhoek's story, *The Chain Around My Neck*, told by the quiet January, whose life appears less heroic/catastrophic than that of her sister Giselle. Vryenhoek builds this story through revelation of character, and the voice of January holds the reader as a confidante; she gradually lets us in on her own secret cataclysm, far greater than Giselle's. In Sara Tilley's story *Her Adolescence*, language becomes a character in itself, so alive the story writhes with the vitality of the thirteen-year-old protagonist who writes notes her dying mother dictates in a notebook that becomes both hymn and secret prescription for the girl's own glorious survival. Michael Crummey's story *The Night Watchman* intensifies through similar use of a witness, a hyper-observant character who filters the pressure and dark story of a company town called Black Rock. Circumstance, character and detail pressurize this story: Wah Lee who arrives on the Company train, addressed like a parcel so he will arrive in the right town to start a laundry; Stick Walker, stymied in his own hero's path to smalltown hockey stardom and sniffing out someone to blame; Wah Lee's wife, pinned so far beyond lonesome she becomes the whole town's breaking point; Ellen, the narrator's own missed boat to companionship.

There is no companionship here, save what a person can dredge from the heart of his or her own company, and in that sense, like all dark books, *Hard Ol' Spot* is at some level a book about loneliness.

Darkness, to be seen, needs points of contrasting illumination, and illustrator Darren Whalen has given each tale a visual signature in a style that calls to mind illuminations of handmade manuscripts. Whalen presents a sense of story as narrative as the texts he illuminates here. From his calligraphic framing to the dreamlike pen and pencil-painting in each plate, the detail and dynamic atmospherics mirror what the writers have attempted. The sacrificial drudgery in Michelle Butler-Hallett's *Eminent Domain*; the vertigo in Joanne Soper-Cook's *Sky*; the disappointed vulnerability in Elizabeth Blanchard's *Drive Thru*. There is a nod, in these line and shadow pieces, and in the stories, to Poe, to Oscar Wilde, to old craft that involves a quill, an inkpot and a sinister edge.

Rock and water at midnight, an empty beer carton, a broken promise, a lost dream. The brightest sliver of redemption in *Hard Ol' Spot* comes from that place in a writer's toolbox that nails up a board, and on the board is written the question: "Can you face this, or will you turn away?" We have thousands of stories that do turn away; that make life soften, relent, forgive, or melt into gentleness. Then there are those who say the only way to dissolve hard-core pain is to face it, head-on, and that is what these stories try to do.

Break, break, break,
At the foot of thy crags, O Sea!
But the tender grace of a day that is dead
Will never come back to me.
    - Tennyson

The house is trembling, and I can't sleep because every time the wind slams against the side of our bungalow, I feel like bawling. It feels like being violated, over and over. I just wish it would stop.

This has been the worst day of my life. Valentine's Day in Darwin, Newfoundland. 1982. Might as well mark the date in this diary because it's a day to remember, although maybe I'd be better off forgetting it.

Mark came over today. I was in the kitchen by myself, even though I was stuck babysitting my little brother, Stevie, again. He was scared of the gale, like always, and hiding under his bed ever since it started.

BREAK, BREAK, BREAK

"Some bad storm," Mark said and sat down at the kitchen table like he owned the place. "Get us a cup o' tea, would ya? I'm froze to death."

I boiled the kettle and got him his tea. "I heard on the radio that it's s'posed to get worse. Especially out on the Banks."

He looked at me and said not to be talking so foolish. "That rig is unsinkable." He sipped on his tea. "Granted, we've all heard that before. Nothing lasts forever, even when we think it will."

"Thanks for cheering me up." I folded my arms across my chest and started to pace. Even then, in the middle of the afternoon, our rickety old house was shaking once in a while, like a mild earthquake had struck us from beneath the foundation. My father and his brothers had built it about fifteen years ago, and its cheap wooden frame always groaned in heavy wind. A white five-gallon meat bucket in the corner of the kitchen caught the rain that seeped inside. Every ten seconds or so, the bucket would go *plop*! It felt like the storm was coming inside, and I must have looked miserable because Mark was looking at me like I had twenty heads. He kept running a finger across his burnt lip, and I couldn't bear to see him hurt like that. I asked him if I could kiss it to make it better.

He averted his eyes then and would only look at the bucket slowly filling with raindrops. We made small talk about the weather for a few minutes, but he seemed agitated, like he wasn't really there with me. The wind rocked the house again and Stevie called out to me from the bedroom. "I should check on him."

When I stood up, Mark suddenly tested his tea and then gulped it down. "That's all right." He wiped his lips and rose to his feet right quick, like he couldn't wait to get away from me. "I should be going anyway, I s'pose."

"Wait a minute, you." I pulled on the lapels of his parka and pulled him close, trying to give him a hug, but he kept pulling away. "Don't think you can fool me." I grinned at him, but I was getting a little bit nervous. "It's Valentine's Day, you know. And

I know you. You've got a gift or a card or something in them big pockets." I reached into both sides of his coat and rummaged around, but he pulled away again before I could feel anything.

"Well, see, there's the thing." He cleared his throat and looked out the window behind me. The wind howled through the chimney and I thought for sure the whole house would lift off its moorings and fly away. Meanwhile, Stevie bawled out to me again and I had to tell him I'd be there in a minute. Mark sighed patiently.

"I got some bad news that I came here to tell you." His eyes were misty and a bit angry. I knew what he was going to say and asked him not to say it. But he'd screwed up his courage and made himself come so far to deliver the message that it wasn't fair for me, he said, to deny him the chance to just out with it.

"I can't do this anymore." He had a hard time looking at me, and he was doing up his coat and tugging at his stuck zipper, while pulling my world out from under me.

"Please don't, Mark." I tried to put my arms around him, but he pushed me away.

"Don't make this harder. It's not easy for me to do."

"Then don't do it. Just stay with me. I don't have anyone else."

He pulled open the kitchen door and stepped into the porch, turning around to look at me one last time. Meanwhile, the raindrops kept dripping into the meat bucket, making that depressing sound.

I grabbed hold of the knob on my side of the door. "You're breaking my heart." I didn't say it angrily, just incredibly sad, from deep down into my bones. My life was over. It was Valentine's Day and my boyfriend for the last three years was breaking up with me. If he walked out that door, I would be completely alone.

He gripped the doorknob and looked straight at me, and I'll never forget the expression in those steely blue eyes that I've always adored most about him. It was as if he was running for his life, scared of getting trapped by me.

BREAK, BREAK, BREAK

Last time we talked, Friday night down at the snack bar, Mark was really moody. I was playing pool with some girls from school and he was just sitting on a stool in the corner, pretending to be interested. He kept asking me if I was going to be at this all night and so we left earlier than I wanted to. It seemed that, lately, he was always pulling me away from my friends. Still, I never saw it coming. We were walking home, holding hands, when he asked, "Does it ever bother you that I'm a bit older than you?"

"It's only three years." I let go of his hand and halted in my tracks. A steady cold breeze made my eyes water. When he turned to face me, I shrugged and made light of it. "Besides, girls mature faster than boys."

"Not always." Something in the way he said it and the cold, distant look in his eyes when he kissed me goodnight on the front step made me wonder what he meant. "Besides, sometimes I wonder if I'm holding you back."

Two nights later, at the beginning of that vicious storm, he stood in the porch, on the verge of leaving me, and suddenly I knew for sure what he'd been getting at. Mark was never one for words and probably just couldn't say it outright. Sure, I understood, but I often wished he would try a bit harder to explain himself. He thought he was too old for me, keeping me from spending time with friends my own age.

He reached toward me and laid a hand on my cheek. I was trying not to cry, but I couldn't help it. "Someday you'll see that this is not the worst thing in the world that could happen to you."

"Why are you doing this?"

He just shrugged and shook his head mournfully. "Don't ask what you already know the answer to."

"Please don't leave me. I love you."

He wiped one tear from my cheek and withdrew his hand, sticking it in his pocket. He pulled the door shut and was gone. Just like that. I didn't even get a last kiss or a hug. My heart was pounding. My head was spinning. I thought I was going to die on the spot. When Stevie yelled out again, I just sank in a heap in the middle of the kitchen floor and bawled my eyes out until my mother came home from Mass and found me there. When I told her what had happened, she just pulled me up, guiding me into her arms and sat me down at the table. She went in to check on Stevie and, a few minutes later, she came back and sat down across from me, holding my hands.

She didn't say anything, though. It wasn't like my mother to talk very much. She went to church a lot lately, especially since Dad took the job out on the rig last fall. There were two of us kids and, with Mom not working, he had to pay child support, so what choice did he have? "The money is good," I remember him saying. It would mean not seeing me and my little brother very often, just every four weeks. He kept saying that, with a faraway look in his eyes, every time I asked him why he had to go all the way out on the ocean just to find a stupid job.

"With money, you can have a life," he said at Christmas time.

"Aren't there any jobs around here?" I asked. He and Mom weren't even divorced yet, but he was still coming around to see us, to make sure we didn't need anything.

"You find me a good job right here on land and I'll stay." He took me onto his knee and wrapped his arms around me, even though I'm nearly sixteen and getting too big for that. But he never cares about that stuff. He isn't a perfect dad. I think he drinks a little bit and he always seems to be smoking. And he's always swearing around us, which Mom is always warning him about. "I'll do this for a couple of years and make me fortune. Meanwhile, I can take care of you and your brother. Then, I'll come back and build me a great big house right here, just up over the hill with that great ocean view, and we can see each other all the time."

I nodded and smiled, even gave him a squeeze, but he could probably see in my eyes that I didn't believe him. Not much good ever happens in my life, so I don't believe in happy endings, even though I want to.

He stroked my cheek with his rough hand. "Have a little faith, my darling." He didn't even have Christmas dinner with us, even though Mom asked him if he would like to stay. He mumbled something about us probably having more fun without him and then he just left.

I don't know why I was thinking about all of that after Mark broke up with me. Meanwhile, here was my silent, well-meaning mother sitting here and stroking my hand. "It's going to be okay," she finally offered. Then she got up to dump the bucket's contents into the sink and placed it in the corner again without missing a drop. I just sighed, thinking it was the most useless thing she could have said when my life was in shambles and tomorrow wasn't something I could ever look forward to again. Not without Mark. Dad would have painted a picture of what it would be like, of how it would all be better soon. He would have hugged me.

The tears wouldn't stop coming from my eyes, even when Stevie came out from hiding and crawled into my lap, asking me what was wrong. Whenever I thought I was cried out, it would start over, especially when the wind rocked the house again and again. Each time, I just held my little brother tighter and tighter, until I thought we both would break. Now and then, Mom would get up and look out the window, leaning on the sink and clutching the countertop with her fingers, as if she would snap off a chunk of it if she was strong enough.

"I wish Dad was here." It probably sounded like I was accusing her of not being sufficient, and I wished I could take it back the moment I said it.

She just wheeled around and looked at me as if I had broken her heart. She wasn't crying though. I was looking for tears and they just weren't coming. Her eyes were as dry as the Sahara. "I wish he was, too." Her words amazed me, to the point where my tears suddenly stopped, except for the occasional one leaking down from the corner of each eye.

I wonder now what she meant by that. Did she wish he was there always and back living with us? Would she and Dad patch things up when he came home? That would be the best Valentine's gift ever! It would almost make up for Mark being such an idiot. I mean, who breaks up with their girlfriend on Valentine's Day? Now I'm getting angry, the more I think about it. And I find myself wishing that something terrible would happen to him. I used to love Mark, but he hurt me so bad today that I don't think I can ever laugh or smile again. I hope he has an accident. I don't want him to die, but I want him to lie in a hospital bed and wish I would come see him. And then I would be there, stroking his hair and kissing his forehead, not telling him it was me that had wished him such bad luck and probably caused the accident. But he'd see how pretty I am and how good I could have been to him, but now it's too late. "You can't have me," I'd say. "I've moved on."

I often think I can not only see the future, but affect it too. So I know it's wrong to say, but I'm really concentrating now on Mark having something bad happen to him. Something so horrible that he'll have to see how beautiful I am. How much grace I have. How much he's lost.

Now I'm focusing on my dad, out there on the ocean, with the rest of the men. Huge waves are probably battering the side of the *Ranger* and making it rock like it was going to sink. But it won't sink. The waves calm down, in fact. I imagine there's a protective shield over the entire rig, and the snow and freezing rain, the wind and the fog are all on the outside of it, just blowing around this invisible bubble, unable to hurt either the rig or my dad. I know he'll be safe. And the morning will come, and the sun will be shining, and no one will even know that it was me that kept them protected throughout the night. Just me and my little thoughts.

It's not really prayer, though, because me and God aren't exactly on good terms after today. I think God's abandoned me, just like He did with Jesus, when His son needed him most. *Forsaken.* That's the word. And then He just left Jesus to die, and the people were incredibly sad and angry that God the Father could just let His only child be crucified like that. It was almost like they didn't believe it could really happen, especially it being the Passover, and everything. If God is really good, He has a funny way of showing it sometimes.

That's sort of like my mom. She was really restless all day. I mean, I know she loves me and my brother, but she just has a strange way of showing it.

Like tonight, after supper. She just sat around the kitchen table, listening to the radio, getting really somber when the sad country songs came on the radio. Like "Rose Garden" and "Crystal Chandelier". She hummed along with them, but not in a happy voice. Whenever the news report came on, she would turn up the radio and walk over to the kitchen window, looking out to the ocean. Which made no sense to me because, when it's dark, you can't see the ocean from our house, only hear it. And with the wind so loud, you couldn't hear anything else.

Every weather report made her get more antsy. At one point, she started pacing around like a madwoman, wringing her hands in front of her and praying. She pulled her rosary beads from out of her apron pocket and knelt down in front of the sink. "Come, say the rosary with me," she said in a low, scary voice. Instead of arguing, as I usually would have done, I knelt with her and joined my hands. She called out for Stevie to come join us, and when he was kneeling there beside me, rubbing his tired eyes, my mother led us in the rosary. It wasn't fast and meaningless like usual, though. This time, it was slow and deliberate. Terrifying.

Meanwhile, as the water level in our bucket rose, the house shook and groaned as if the clapboard was going to pull away from the exterior, nails and all. And I was deathly afraid that the house would fall apart and leave the three of us kneeling there by the sink, while the wind and rain and snow lashed at us from all sides.

One particular blast struck the house with such brutal force that we clung to each other to keep from falling to one side. I held tight to Stevie, especially, and when the gust had passed over, my mother stopped praying and slowly stood up. She grabbed her boots and coat from the porch, and told us to do the same while she was pulling on her outdoor clothes.

My brother asked, "Where are we going?" But my silent mother ignored our questions while she dumped and replaced the rain bucket.

She hustled us outdoors into the wildest February night I have ever seen, and I couldn't help but wonder where Mark was and who he was with. I wondered if it was really over between us. Just because he said it, didn't mean anything. Men often say things they don't mean. Mom says that men are natural-born liars and they'd say anything to get you to do what they wanted. But I'm not sure I believe her. I'm not certain of anything anymore. To tell the truth, I think most men actually believe the things they are saying. That way, they don't have to lie.

She shunted us into the car, with the rain and snow pelting down on our windshield in big sploshy drops and wet, splashy flakes. We've got a crappy old Chevette in which the wipers don't work right—the blades were so worn out that they could barely clear a space in the windshield. I don't know how she could see anything. Every now and again, big gusts of wind would seize the car and make it rattle, like it was going to run us off the road and into a ditch.

It was the longest ten minutes of my life, and I honestly didn't think we'd make it home alive.

She drove out on the dirt road to the Point, and suddenly, I knew why she had taken us there.

"Stay in the car," she told us, and I had no argument with that. The Point is just outside of town and it's mostly young people who go there to drink or neck, or whatever. It's just this skinny bit of land that sticks out into the North Atlantic, and it's not a place where you'd want to be on a stormy night. So, truthfully, I feared for her sanity. She looked tired and worn at the edges, with a look in her eyes that made me think she had spent the whole day staring at the one thing for too long, like I used to do when I was studying for exams before Christmas. I wished I could reach out to her, to do something for her, to at least

BREAK, BREAK, BREAK

make the storm relent and leave us alone, so that we could all go back to normal.

I was also worried about my baby brother. This must all be so weird and horrible to him, to have his mother acting like a crazy woman in the middle of a winter hurricane and his big sister brooding and crying her eyes out all day. I sat him on my lap and held him tight in my arms, rocking back and forth. "It's going to be okay," I said, turning on the radio to some soft country song. "We'll go home again soon and everything will be fine. The wind will stop, and Mom will calm down, and we'll all go to sleep."

"Okay," he said and, within moments, he was dozing in my arms.

Through the windshield, I watched my mother make her way onto the point. The rain and snow obscured my view, but the wind was mostly just sweeping the water across the glass landscape, allowing me to see her through a foggy glaze.

She didn't go all the way out to the edge, because that would have been suicide. Even in the dark, I could see the gigantic waves smashing against the rocks, trying to pull the entire cliff out into the sea, all in one huge grab. My mother was a good ways off from the car, where I sat. She almost seemed to be enjoying the feel of the wind through her body, even though it threatened to take her away. It was like she wanted to let go of the earth and surrender herself to whatever was going to come. I knew, because I was having that same feeling myself, like my insides were in knots and all I wanted to do was just curl up and go to sleep forever. She leaned slightly towards a massive boulder to her left, her hair flying in tangles towards her face.

My gaze followed hers. She was looking out to sea, presumably in the direction of my father, where he probably clung to a bunk, like everyone else on board, riding out the storm, wishing and praying that it was over. Just like we were. But the longer my mother stood there, the more worried I got. A vision flashed in my mind, so dark and disturbing, so hopelessly violent, that I can't even write it down. Even now, as I think about it, I just want to get down on my knees and vomit. I became so scared that I started to pray out loud in a whisper, "Our Father who art in Heaven. Hallowed be thy name." I couldn't remember it all. Strange, because I knew it by heart. But, for some reason, my rote memory failed me. So I skipped around to words I could grasp onto: "Thy kingdom come, thy will be done, on earth as it is in heaven."

My mother stood beside that rock, one hand gripping its edge to keep her from blowing forward. It was then I realized how dangerous it was for her. I blew the horn several times as a warning, but she didn't seem to hear it. The wind was just howling and screeching all around us. I actually feared the car would tip over and tumble down over the rocks and into the sea.

My mother suddenly turned back towards the Chevette, gripping the front collar of her jacket closed with one hand and covering her face with the other to protect it from the bitter cold and driving rain.

"It's enough to cut you in two," was all she said when she got in the car. She had to struggle to keep the door from blowing off its hinges before she finally got it shut. When she clicked off the radio, we both sat there for a few moments, looking out at the awesome waves. Stevie was snoring gently, his arms still wrapped around my neck.

"He'll be okay." It was all I could think of to say. I felt just as much anguish as she did. I loved her more than ever in that moment because I could tell how much she loved my father. Even if they couldn't be together in the same house. "The radio says the storm should let up a bit in the morning."

She laid a cold hand on my lap. "That'll be some good news anyway."

Then she drove us home without another word between us. Somehow, though, by the time I crawled into bed in that tiny bungalow, I felt that things were better between me and her.

As I write this, I actually have a little bit of hope inside of me that everything will be okay. Maybe Mark and I can patch things up tomorrow. I'm sure he still loves me. He's just confused, that's all. It's the storm and the time of year. Valentine's Day can make everything seem so much worse than it is, even if things are pretty bad.

He did break my heart though and I'm not sure I'll ever get over that. It's the worst thing that could have happened to me, on this day of all days, and with Mom going out of her mind with worry about Dad, she wasn't even able to comfort me at all. I feel bad for her, but I really needed her today. Dad is always the one I turn to, and I hate that he's always away, especially nights like this.

Mom will feel better in the morning too. She'll stop worrying, and so will I, and we'll go back to our routine. I'll get up and go to school. I'll talk to my friends and we'll fool around and make fun of the teachers, and if the weather is good, we'll all meet up at the snack bar tomorrow night. I could use some company right now.

Jesus! There goes the wind again. Just now, the loudest gust of wind I have ever heard slammed into the side of the house like a bomb went off. I've got actual tears coming from my eyes and falling onto the page. I know it's only the wind, but I wish it would stop. I hope Stevie's okay, though I don't hear him. I wonder if Mom remembered to dump the meat bucket. God, I want this storm to be over! I might even pray again tonight.

Now I lay me down to sleep, I pray the Lord my soul to keep. If I should die before I wake, I pray the Lord my soul to take.

I'm signing off now. I'm laughing suddenly at that morbid prayer and Mom just yelled out to ask if I was crying. Some day, years from now, I'm sure I'll be reading my diary for this night and I'll laugh at how silly and scared I was. Just a childish little girl who wants her daddy. Tomorrow, everything will look different.

Thank God for that.

DRIVE-THRU

ELIZABETH BLANCHARD

"**D**ecaffeinated tea, large with two cream, remove the bag." Penny presses her finger against the earpiece to better hear the male voice, a discreet act of intimacy that makes her smile while she punches the keys of the cash register.

"One forty, drive up to the window please."

Her own voice comes at her through the headset, sounds strange, not her own. She imagines a grey-haired lump of a man leaning out of his car window, his head cocked to one side in the dark, straining to hear her commands. The small black microphone arches in front of her mouth, moves with her head, makes her feel essential as though she were connected to some significant event. Digital red numbers flash at the corner of the brightly lit window counting the seconds.

"You gonna close up tonight, Penny?" Chazz smiles as he carries out another tray of donuts through the swinging door, the last batch of the day. His hair net much too visible against his brown hair, the seam of which creates a vertical axis with the gap between his front teeth. Everything about Chazz is broad, his shoulders, his laugh, his nose. His back-slap friendliness is too loud, too open; he has none of that dark allure Penny has noticed in other boys, in other men.

Penny's aunt, who never married, always said that Chazz would be a good catch. "Honest, dependable, faithful." I could always get a dog, was Penny's first thought on hearing her aunt's comments, but she never said it out loud, for it wouldn't do to say such things to her aunt.

Penny adds another bag of milk to the dispenser, the large pouch folding awkwardly under the pressure of her thin fingers. Her mind wanders and she imagines what it would be like if her breasts were full of milk. Her feet are hot in her sneakers. Chazz tells all the girls that open-toe sandals are not permitted. Penny doesn't mind; she never wears sandals anymore. Her toes are webbed. Not all of them of course, just between the second and third, on each foot. She wears socks, even in the summer, white ones with the grey heel and toe. The kind of socks that leave the skin ribbed around the ankle. At night, Penny sits on the edge of her bed, rests her chin on her knees, and runs her fingers over the tiny ridges of skin just above the ankle bone. She remembers her grandmother's house on the Island and the rolling banks of sand, wind-rippled and holding the heat of a July sun long into the evening. Back then, Penny would spend the entire summer barefoot; there was never any mention of her toes, as though irregularities of the sort went unnoticed on the Island, were inherent to the landscape.

Penny met Chazz the year her grandmother died and she took the ferry to the mainland to come to live on the edge of town with her grandmother's sister, Aunt Margaret. Chazz lived on the other side of the road from Aunt Margaret's place and crossed over the day after Penny arrived. "What's wrong with your toes?" He asked, obtrusively pointing to Penny's thonged feet, "you're like a duck." Years later, he would invite Penny to his graduation dance in the same boisterous manner. "I'm stuck for a date", he said with a braggart smile in front of a table full of pimpled-faced boys in the school cafeteria, his huge hand coming down on her back, as though sharing some off-color joke between pals. Penny accepted only because she was two years younger than Chazz and wanted go to a seniors' dance. This is what she would tell herself later.

A flush of embarrassment still comes over Penny at the thought of the peach-colored dress Aunt Margaret pulled out from the garment bag in the back of her closet. The material was light and the skirt floated in layers of gauzy chiffon, one longer than the next, until the layer closest to her skin drifted down below her knees. Penny stood on a chair in the kitchen as Aunt Margaret, straight pins pinched between her lips, spoke of the Saturday night ceilidh on the Island in wistful tones as her bony fingers tugged sharply at the waistline; Penny being fitted into Aunt Margaret's memory. Her aunt surprised the girl with closed-toe sandals.

At the dance, Penny spent most of her evening leaning against a long table covered with scalloped-edge sandwiches shaved of their crusts. After the first half-hour, realizing nobody had noticed her, she imagined herself invisible and forgot about the dress she was wearing. Having resisted Chazz's many offers to dance, Penny watched him as he wiggled his way into the circle of short-skirted girls dancing at the center of the gym, rolling his huge shoulders like a disco bull, unmindful of the raised eyebrows and sly smiles.

And there is still the memory of the dark-eyed boy who squeezed by to talk to the blond girl standing next to Penny, whiffs of cigarette smoke and warm alcohol on his breath, his mouth touching the girl's hair while leaning in close, his voice husky and low. His elbow pushed up against Penny's ribs as he placed his hand on the small of the girl's back. Penny's eyes followed the couple as they left through the side door, the boy's black suit disappearing quickly into the night, the red of the girl's dress lingering. A wave of cool air washed back into the gym across the dance floor where Chazz's hips and shoulders rode the wave of music, a stiff low beat resonating under Penny's breastbone.

DRIVE-THRU

Why she let Chazz kiss her that night, his tongue thick and awkward, his mouth cavernous, Penny really can't say; his large damp hand fumbling under the layers of her aunt's peach chiffon, the taste of egg and tuna sandwiches on his tongue.

***

"Do you have any Sour-Cream Glazed today?" Penny recognizes the voice. She raises her head, looks over to where Chazz is changing the coffee filters in one of the machines.

"Sorry, we're all out of Sour-Cream Glazed," Penny answers into her headset, feeling the heat rise to her face.

"Well," the voice says rolling the 'l's a little longer than needed. "What's left?"

Penny looks over the half empty trays and starts from the left to the right.

"Double Chocolate, Boston Cream," her heart feels like it's rolling down a hill, picking up speed. "Old-fashion Sugar, Old-fashion Plain, Maple Dip", Chazz is sweeping the floor around her feet. "Vanilla Sprinkle, Honey Dip, Toffee Glazed," she pauses, covers the mouthpiece with one hand, and runs the other down the front of her khaki shirt, which has a coffee stain just above her navel.

"Any others?" the voice is right in her ear. It sounds as though it's pressed against the box. How the hell does he do that? Does he open the door and get out, or does he actually drive up onto the lip of grass?

"That's all."

"Any muffins?"

"Yes."

Another pause.

"What kind?" He's playing the game; he always does.

"Blueberry, Bran, Carrot," she knows that he only wants a coffee. "Chocolate Chip, Low-fat Cranberry", he'll ask for black with two sugars. "Fruit Explosion and Berry-Burst," only he won't say black, he'll say dark.

He sometimes waits for her, after closing. Penny recognizes his car at the back of the parking lot, near the dirt road that leads through the trailer park. She can see his arm hanging out of the car window.

"I'll have a coffee," he says "large, with two sugar."

He waits for the question.

"Cream or milk?"

"Dark, please."

She knows he is called Rick and that his hair is straight and black, long enough to tuck behind his ears. His skin is rough, raw; maybe he's older than she imagines him to be. As he drives up to the window, she is slow pouring the coffee, hoping that he'll already have put the change on the window's edge when she turns, but he hasn't.

"That'll be one-fourty, please." Palm up, Penny sticks her hand out the window. Tonight he's wearing a white shirt, sleeves pushed back, there's a button missing and the collar isn't pressed.

He carefully wraps his fingers around her wrist and gives a slight tug, dropping the coins in her palm, one at a time.

Penny's ribs feel tight, like her heart is beating in too small a space. She makes no attempt to pull her arm back; she imagines herself being yanked into the car, her breast pulled across his white shirt, her knees coming down hard onto his lap, the smell of his breath.

"Remind me to post the new schedule tomorrow, Penny." Chazz is now standing behind her, zipping his jacket, his shift done for the night.

The man called Rick lets her wrist slide between his fingers, turns up the music, smiles at her through slanted eyes then drives away slowly.

Chazz leans over Penny's shoulder and points to the cup, hot in her hand. "Did he just forget his coffee?"

When they were younger, Aunt Margaret used to pay Chazz three dollars an hour to help with the yard work. He's a good

DRIVE-THRU

worker, that boy, she would tell Chazz's mother in a loud voice, then wink when he wasn't looking.

"Who did you live with before you moved here?" Chazz was raking the mud-colored leaves from under the front porch; still damp with the spring melt, their edges brittle and frayed, rustling under the scratch of the rake.

Waves of white cotton sheets billowed in the wind, ballooning up under Penny's armpits as she groped for the clothespins on the line above her head. Aunt Margaret liked to hang the clothes as early as possible in the spring.

"My grandmother, on the Island." Penny let another clothespin drop into the plastic ice cream container next to her feet.

"Why didn't you stay with her?"

"She died."

"Where are your parents?" Chazz continued in his own graceless manner as he squatted to look under the steps. "Why aren't you living with your folks?"

The muscles in Penny's shoulders tightened. Did he have to talk so loud?

"Are you an orphan?"

Even at eleven years old, Penny knew someone like Chazz, who had lived his entire life in the same house with his parents, could not understand how it could be any other way without a whole lot of explanation.

"Are your folks dead? Car accident or something?"

And the explaining changed things, it always did, it changed the listener. Her grandmother knew this, that's why she never asked Penny about what went on before Penny came to live with her. She never even asked the night Penny stood in the porch light holding a white plastic bag stuffed with her panties, socks and t-shirts, and a naked Barbie-doll; its legs sticking out of the bag in the shape of a hard 'V'.

"Go on, honey," her mother had said earlier, leaning out of the open window of the car door in her grandmother's driveway, gently patting Penny's behind, pointing to her grandmother's front steps, her mother's red fingernails and copper colored bracelets aglow in the headlights of the car. "Go up and knock on Grandma's door." The words sounded funny, as if her mother's tongue were coated with batter.

Penny couldn't see Jim, her mother's friend, behind the wheel, just the flare of his cigarette in the dark, and the sweet-sick smell of the pomade he spread on his hair in front of the mirror every day to make it look shiny.

"Go, sweetie, just knock on the door and Grandma'll let you in."

Penny squinted when the porch light came on and her grandmother opened the door. When she heard the car pull out of the driveway, she checked an impulse to turn and look, for fear of that feeling, the feeling of hovering too close to the edge of something.

Years later, at her grandmother's funeral, when Aunt Margaret whispered to her in church that they couldn't locate her parents and that she would come live with her, Penny wasn't sure if the fluttering inside her stomach was disappointment or relief. She kept her eyes fixed on the brass fittings in which the men from town slid their thick hands and carried the coffin up the aisle. One of the men limped, as though her grandmother were too heavy.

***

"Large coffee, black."

It's a woman's voice this time, tight and clipped, probably like her hair. Penny imagines an expensive knit sweater in a neutral tone, a carefully pressed knee-length skirt under a forest green London Fog overcoat. The richly embroidered scarf Penny pictures looped around the woman's neck is the only drama the woman allows herself. As the Audi moves out of the shadows up to the window, the woman turns on the ceiling light and rifles impatiently through her purse for loose change. The color of the overcoat is grey and the scarf, much lighter than expected, almost translucent, is lying on the seat next to the woman, as if it belongs to someone else. A brisk gust of wind, thinks Penny, and it's gone.

They drove to the Island the summer after Penny's graduation. It was Aunt Margaret's idea. Chazz had been working at Tim Hortons for almost three years, had just been named manager, and had finally paid off his second-hand silver Toyota Tercel. One could hardly tell where he touched up the rust spots.

Aunt Margaret insisted that she sit in the back seat. Every time she came across some familiar sight, she slid forward and stuck her arm out over Penny's shoulder like a crossing guard and pointed.

"Fox Creek; your grandmother and I went to school there, a 45-minute walk every single day. Lordee! Winters were cold. There's old McPherson's farm. Beth MacKie tells me his grandson sold it last year."

They rented a cabin near where Penny's grandmother used to live. Aunt Margaret and Penny shared the bedroom, Chazz slept on a pull-out in the living room. Days were spent on the beach. Aunt Margaret dozed under the parasol, the wide brim of her straw hat popping up and back in the wind, while Chazz knelt in the wet sand and dug collapsing holes with his thick fingers, fishing out bar clams the size of his palm, the smooth white shells streaked blue by the sea.

When Chazz proposed, Penny was sitting on the sand dune, barefeet, her webbed toes dug deep into red clay. In hindsight, Penny often wonders if it wasn't the relentless wash of the waves that eroded her judgment. Before supper, in the quiet of the cabin, the salt water having left traces of white on her skin, Penny showed Aunt Margaret the ring with its speck of a stone that barely glittered. Holding the girl's finger up to the light to see better, her aunt dropped her shoulders and sighed as though the weight of an unfulfilled promise had just been lifted. That night, Penny lay in the dark next to Aunt Margaret trying to remember if she had actually said yes.

***

"Wanna get in?" the man called Rick asks, his arm hangs loosely out the car door window, the white of his sleeve strangely bright against the dark hair on his forearm.

Penny is standing a few feet away from his car, her heart is pounding stone. She wasn't going to walk over. The plan was that she would wait for Chazz in front of the Tim Hortons, under the street light, not at the back of the parking lot. But when she finished her shift and stepped out the back door to put the garbage out, she saw his car near the dirt road that led through the empty field at the back of the parking lot. Chazz was late; Rick called her over. She did not respond, pretending not to hear. But then he called her again; she liked the sound of him making its way to her in the dark, appealing to something in her, a stray memory.

"Well?" he says, in that slow voice, dragging the 'l's as though he were angling for something under the surface.

"I'm engaged." Penny is embarrassed by the lack of conviction in her voice, how feeble the argument sounds in her throat.

He smiles, "You don't have to if you don't want to…" His teeth are white, no gap, his eyes are dark. Stretching his arm across the seat, he opens the passenger door while keeping his eyes on Penny, who has an urge to finger the buttons on his shirt, draw smooth small circles with her thumb. He reaches out and runs the tip of his finger down her wrist, then lets his hand fall, the thud of his knuckles against the car door. The blood-rush swells her eardrums, she imagines his hands on her skin; his fingers are slender. She wonders if his hipbones are as lean. She is certain that he would not close his eyes when moving in against her, when kissing her. He would look at her, like he is now. In the darkness of the parking lot, the smell of oil and dust rising out from under the car, Penny lets herself slip into the stream. She walks around the car and lowers herself onto the seat. He begins to lean towards her to close the door

DRIVE-THRU

when the sound of a horn shrieks through the night air. It's Chazz, parked out front. Penny grabs the handle on the door. The stranger stops. His hand on the dash, he turns his head towards the sound, then looks at Penny.

"What d'ya wanna do?"

His body doesn't quite fill in his shirt, the white cotton hangs loosely around his waist. For the first time in a long time, Penny thinks of her mother, has a fleeting glimpse of how it must have been, that night in her grandmother's driveway.

"Just don't turn on the headlights, ok," Penny says, quietly closing the door.

She rolls up her window as they back out of the parking lot onto the dirt road, resists a wild urge to remove her sneakers and socks, and concentrates on the sound of stones crushing under the tires.

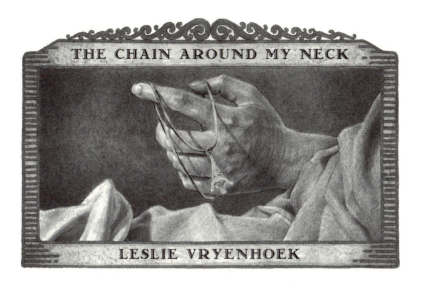

THE CHAIN AROUND MY NECK

LESLIE VRYENHOEK

When she was seven, walking home from school, some guy waved my sister Giselle over to his car so he could show her he was wanking off. She came home totally freaked out, and of course Mom freaked out, too, and called the police. And then she called Dad and told him to come home—this was when he still lived here—and while the police talked to Giselle, Mom flapped around, her hands doing that fluttery thing at the end of her bracelets. When she saw me standing in the doorway of the living room where they were all huddled, she told me, "Never mind, go back to the kitchen. Your sister saw a bad man, that's all. Do your homework."

Like, at nine, I wouldn't figure out what they were talking about. Like the same thing hadn't happened to me and half my friends by then. I couldn't see what the big deal was, but I think we got pizza that night to reward Giselle for living through the ordeal.

It's been non-stop since then. It's like Giselle's attracted to trouble as much as it's attracted to her. But she's got the

THE CHAIN AROUND MY NECK

innocent thing down pat—she always acts like she was just walking along, going about her business when wham, trouble smacked right into her and knocked her down.

Crisis after crisis, as Mom says: Giselle's bored and demanding at school; Giselle's acting out because she misses your dad; Giselle's sick with some kind of gut-eating disease. For two weeks, I had to go to all her classes and gather her homework and take it to the hospital every night, like missing a day of Grade 8 was going to kill her faster than bacteria.

One day, I got tired of how heavy my backpack was, and I said to one of her teachers, "Why does she need to do all this homework? She's dying anyway," which was a total lie because unlike the week before, Mom wasn't even crying all the way to the hospital and all the way home while I tried to pretend to read a book, so I knew Giselle must be getting better. Still, it worked; the teachers stopped giving me her assignments. Instead, they started saying, "You tell Giselle we're thinking about her, and we just want her to get better."

When she came back to school completely alive, they all just about burst an artery piling the catch-up work on her.

And before she'd even gained enough weight so she didn't look tragically wasted, she slept over at a friend's and the house burned down. And there was Giselle, flinging her friend and her skinny self out a second-storey window. Apparently, it was her idea to throw the pillows and bean bag chairs out first, and she got the credit for saving the day and got her picture on the front page of *The Telegram* and people clapped—they actually *clapped* for her—at the school assembly when it got mentioned the next week.

I didn't clap. I mean, really, how much brainpower does it take to think to throw a few pillows onto the lawn before you jump out a window? And when my friend Anna saw I wasn't clapping, she stopped clapping, too—which is one of the things I've liked about her since she sat next to me in Grade 9: Anna gets it. Not like our friend Sheila, who was all affronted: "January! Why aren't you clapping for your sister? She's a hero!"

That's right. My name is January. And, no, to the question everyone asks: I wasn't born in January. I was supposed to be, and Mom and Dad had decided on the name and, then, I was almost two weeks late, but Mom apparently thought it was a great name anyway. Different and dynamic, a real self-starter of a name—she's told me that at least a thousand times. She says they didn't want me to be another Amanda or Ashley or Jessica, so now I'm some freak who spends half her life explaining she was born in February, a freak named after a month that was gone before she even arrived, but that manages to come back every New Year with a big bang.

Fun at parties. I'll bet that's what they were thinking when they named me.

They should have named me something that meant "studies hard so she can get the hell out of here," because that's all I've ever really wanted to do. All through high school, I worked my ass off to get top grades, and I won all the French oration competitions in the province. Not that I cared about the *accomplishment*, which is a big word with the teachers and also with other parents. I wasn't under pressure from home to succeed like some kids I know—I don't think anyone at home was even noticing—I was just looking for a chance to get into university and far, far away from my family.

Besides, what else would I be doing? It's not like guys were clamoring around, wanting to go out with me. If a boy called our house, well, you could be pretty sure he was calling for Giselle. And don't think that didn't generate an overwrought evening or two around here.

While Giselle was socializing up a storm, I was head down, hatching my escape plan.

Eyes on the prize, my dad used to say.

So far, it's working. Next year, I'll start university on a full scholarship and I'll major in French. In just a couple of years, there's a good chance I can study at Paris-Sorbonne, and I've only been totally obsessed with the idea since I saw a brochure about it a few years ago. I've been reading everything I could

THE CHAIN AROUND MY NECK

get my hands on about Paris. I swear, I can walk the streets in my mind already, and I don't even care if Paris is full of dog shit, like people say. Men in Paris appreciate women, and I figure by the time I get there, I'll know how to wear my hair and makeup and how to dress so I don't look so stiff and dumpy. I plan to start making up for lost time.

Eyes on the prize. I have that written on the mirror above my dresser in electric blue marker, and when Mom washes it off in one of her cleaning frenzies, I just write it again, bigger every time.

Mom says I'm too serious or else too driven, and that I'll burn out or give myself ulcers, but she's just not seeing the big picture: Paris is far away from Mount Pearl and far away from Giselle and her problems. And also from Mom, who is completely hooked into the psychodrama of it. It's like Giselle's crises feed some need they both have, and neither of them can see a reason to try to avoid any of it.

One night a couple of years ago, Giselle was out with friends and Mom ordered a ham and pineapple pizza—my favourite, and one that makes Giselle gag, just for effect—and we sat on the floor watching a movie, kind of leaning against each other and chewing. Everything was so perfect. Then Mom said, "Gee, I guess this is how it would be all the time if I'd stopped at one kid."

It was so typical that she would open her mouth and wreck everything. Part of me couldn't believe she'd say something like that and just completely erase one of her kids. Another part of me couldn't believe she was sitting there with me but thinking about Giselle and all her problems.

That was one of the things that made me call Dad and ask if I could come out to Alberta, where he works now, and live with him. I tried to tell him how insane Mom and Giselle were—not that he should need any explanation—and he said, "Don't talk about your mother like that. She deserves your respect."

A few minutes later, when I was already starting to cry (although maybe he couldn't guess that over the phone, and I didn't want him to anyway), he said, "I need you to stay there and look after those two. They're not strong like you are."

I think he just likes being free, not having to worry what his kids are up to. He didn't even come home for Christmas last year; although, he did send me and Giselle nice fat cheques on top of the one he sends Mom every month.

I spent half of mine on clothes, and the other half on CDs. Mom was thrilled that I spent it all, instead of banking it. She loved that it was *so typically teenaged*. I didn't bother to tell her that it was all about prepping for Paris.

The last thing I bought with my Christmas cash was this silver Eiffel Tower charm, which I always wear on a chain around my neck so that whenever things get too crazy, I can hold onto it to remind myself that, just like Dad, I'm getting the hell out of here.

Anyway, the idea of respecting Mom seems pretty laughable. She's nice enough, but totally clueless. She doesn't figure out the most obvious things, like that night when she was at dress rehearsal and Giselle and her friend drank almost an entire bottle of vodka. Giselle fell down the stairs and later puked her guts out and I had to stand behind her at the toilet and hold her hair back and bring her cold water and get her to bed.

The next morning, Mom thought Giselle had the stomach flu. When the vodka ran out, Mom just bought another bottle, like she thought it had evaporated or something. She's always been terrible at keeping track of stuff, and that's when I realized she wouldn't notice if alcohol started disappearing. Which I guess is one favour Giselle did for me along the way.

Giselle had plenty of little crises too; like, when she got caught holding the smashed pieces down by that whole row of birdhouses along the duck pond. They started yelling at her for destroying it, and she started arguing that she'd found it like that and was trying to gather up the pieces to save them.

I remember she came slamming in the door and told the whole story to Mom in tearful indignation, and I was waiting for Mom to say, "Well, *did you* break the birdhouse? Do you know who did?" Instead, Mom got so equally indignant I was afraid she'd call the police again and report a couple of mean old people who'd yelled at the wrong kid.

After that one, things went along swimmingly for, oh, about six minutes before Giselle got pounded in the schoolyard. That was just last winter, right before my Grade 12 midterms and right after I'd started my job at the card store in the mall. I was at work when the principal's office called me to come and pick up Giselle. It made sense, I guess—I had the car, and Mom was rehearsing, so no one wanted to bother her. Even my boss was okay about it. Still, it meant I had to be the one to make the call from Health Sciences and freak Mom out yet again.

There were X-rays and bruises and a sling, and the police came that time, too.

I never did find out what Giselle said to those girls to make them attack. I didn't get to go to court and hear their side of it, since it was during school hours, but I think they pretty much had to plead guilty because of all the witnesses who would have been flapping around like always, trying to help Giselle.

I figure Giselle probably didn't say anything to start the fight. She wouldn't have to. I bet she just raised one eyebrow in that way she has that makes me want to pound the crap out of her, too, except I never do, because I'm the good kid.

It was right after court that Mom decided to take Giselle and go to England for the whole summer. She had relatives she hadn't seen in ages, and some theatre work with an old castmate that I imagine wasn't as big a thing as she made out to her friends on the phone.

"You're old enough to be on your own for awhile. And anyway, Jan," Mom said, because apparently even she can't bear to speak my whole name anymore, "I'm sensing some hostility in you that I think you need to work through."

That's Mom for you. She's always *sensing* things. God forbid she should just ask.

Although, sometimes, I'm glad she doesn't, like when she sensed I was sad because I was keeping a straight face when I drove them to the airport so I wouldn't give away my absolute ecstasy at the thought of two whole months without them.

Waiting for Mom to call from Heathrow, so I could be sure there was a whole ocean between us, almost killed me. I had visions of Giselle deciding to get in some kind of trouble at security or getting assaulted in the bathroom at Halifax airport, and them calling off the whole trip and coming home. But they made it after all, and now this is my reward for putting up with living in the perpetual shadow of Giselle: two whole, uninterrupted months of peace and quiet.

Peace, when I leave for work at the mall, and quiet when I get home. In the evenings, Anna comes over to watch movies and sometimes we pour a drink, try different things from Mom's liquor supply, and then Anna goes home. Her house has a pool and better food in the fridge, and she hasn't had a reason to be out of bed before noon since we graduated. Her parents are totally paying her way, she says, and she gets enough peace and quiet at home since they both go to work early in the morning, and she's an only child. But she's still nice, and not as self-involved as you might expect with that set-up.

Mom and Giselle had been gone thirty-two days, just past the halfway mark, when I got that postcard. It was the third one they'd sent, but this one wasn't from some quaint little English town.

Hey sis! Guess where we are? Paris! Can you believe it?! Mom found a cheap flight and said we just had to go. I hope you get here 'cuz you're right—it's amazing!

I ripped that glossy Eiffel Tower postcard in half, and then into tiny little pieces and I threw them all in the toilet. Then I flushed, and that's exactly when I decided to have the party.

It wasn't like I wanted to get back at Mom and Giselle by wrecking the place—although that did cross my mind. I just wanted something to happen. I wanted to shake right out of myself, to stop always doing exactly the right and expected thing. I wanted something interesting to happen to me, just for once.

Besides, there was this guy, Matt, from the music store at the mall. I had a huge crush on him, and although he seemed way cooler than me and ran with a completely different crowd, he always looked interested in the CDs I bought. I figured having a party was about my best and only shot at him.

So it wouldn't look too obvious, I made invitations on the computer and handed them around to all the people I sort of knew in the stores. That way, I could just casually hand one to Matt—"Oh hey, I'm having a party if you want to come"—while I was buying another CD.

Then Anna invited everybody she thought would come, too, which amounted to about nine people, since we've never been what you would call popular. She told them to bring anyone else they wanted, and she even got her 19-year-old cousin Jeff to get the beer and some tequila for shooters. I cashed my whole paycheque and gave it to him.

I could just picture it, how exciting I would seem when Matt showed up and there was a big party and I had some awesome music cranked. How he would look over at me and see I was more than just some card store clerk.

And then almost nobody showed up. At ten o'clock, there was still just me and Anna, Jeff and his girlfriend, whose name I can never remember, and two girls who work in the Food Court. It was so lame, and I was pissed off and embarrassed and trying really hard not to cry in frustration over my complete inability to generate any excitement whatsoever.

"If Giselle was here, I bet the windows would be smashed out and the cops would be here by now." At least that got a laugh out of Anna.

By this time, I'd stopped going to look out the front window every time I heard a car door slam.

At 10:30, the Food Court babes thought they remembered they were supposed to be somewhere else, and as they were leaving, the one with the ponytail actually said, "Thanks so much for inviting us. I had a really good time!"

I wanted to punch her straight teeth crooked, but I just said, "Sure. See ya around."

Then I drained my beer and put my head with my perfectly straightened hair down on my perfectly ripped jeans—those two things had taken me all afternoon to get right—and I moaned.

Jeff took pity. "Hey, this is cool, and there's plenty of beer to go around. Why don't we just put on a movie and chill." Which was really nice of him, considering how much it looked like he and his girlfriend wanted to go somewhere and rip each other's clothes off.

I was just coming back into the living room with a movie and another beer when Matt and two other guys appeared on the front steps. The sight of them sent me into a total panic. It was almost worse, Matt showing up at my lame non-party, than having him not show up at all.

"Hey January," he said, but his face was saying, "Where the hell is everybody?"

"Hey Matt! Um. There were some other people here earlier but there's some other party that everyone had to go to or something, so, um, anyway, there's lots of beer. Yeah. Come on in."

Anna, because she is totally hooked in and it's like she can read my mind, like she's the only person in the whole world who understands anything, headed for the stereo the second she saw Matt and put on one of the CDs I'd bought to impress him.

I grabbed some beers and passed them around fast to Matt and the other guys, who turned out to be Vince and Riley. I figured if they had one, they might stay for two, and maybe a bunch more people would miraculously appear. Then we all just sat around for a while with the music blaring and me yelling out dumb things like, "So how's work, Matt?"

Vince got up and started walking around the house, picking up stuff and looking at it. He had thick arms that he held

THE CHAIN AROUND MY NECK

out funny from his sides, and black hair so curly it reminded me of a pot scrubber. Everything he picked up he put down in a totally different place. He went all the way through to the kitchen doing that, and then he must have motioned to the other guys because they got up and followed him. The CD had ended, so suddenly it was quiet.

"He totally creeps me out," Anna whispered, and Jeff's girlfriend nodded, which is about as much as she ever seems to do.

I chugged the rest of my beer just so I'd have an excuse to go in there and find out what they were doing, but before I even got to the kitchen, I could hear Vince.

"Hey fucker, I thought you said this was an upscale party we were going to, good drugs and rich booty looking for action. This sucks. Let's get the hell out of here."

"Yeah. What the hell did I know? I was just going by what the bitch wears every day."

"She's kinda hot, but her ugly friend seems totally uptight. Not much of a two-for-one." That was Riley, who looked like a total loser himself—no chin and shiny skin. I looked behind to make sure Anna couldn't hear.

"Okay, well let's get out of here." That was Matt, and my heart just dropped. I put on my game face—that's another saying of Dad's—and stepped around and into the kitchen. If I wanted any chance at all with Matt, I figured I'd better keep his friends happy.

"Anybody up for tequila shots?"

I poured big shots into juice glasses, which wasn't easy since I was already pretty hammered. We all threw back a couple, and then I went back into the living room with the bottle, but only Anna was left. She was looking at me weird.

"Hey Anna, want some tequila?" I held the bottle out to her.

"January, you should stop. You are getting way too drunk."

I couldn't believe how uptight she was being. "What the fuck, are you my mother now? Oh, no, you can't be—my mother's in Paris with Giselle. Because Giselle gets everything. She gets all the attention. She gets trips to Paris. She got to go to counsellors," I drank some tequila straight from the bottle. "No one asked me if I wanted to go to a fucking counsellor. But you wouldn't understand. You get everything handed to you on a fucking platter, too."

Anna stood up, looking really pissed off.

"Fuck off, Anna." I yelled it, but it was too late because she'd already left, slamming the front door behind her.

"Looks like all your little friends are gone but us." Vince was standing behind me. "Hey, you look really wasted. Why don't you let us help you up to bed."

"I don't want to go to bed. Let's have some more tequila." I tried to tip the bottle back up to my lips, but missed, dumping tequila all down my shirt just in time for Matt and Riley to see. All three of them laughed, so I did, too. Vince held his hand out for the bottle. I stumbled just passing it to him, and he took hold of my arm.

"Okay, come on. Let's get you upstairs." He said it like he was really concerned. Like he'd just adopted me as his little sister.

I smiled at Matt. "I'm sorry. I guess I invited you to a really dumb party, but I'm glad you came."

Matt shrugged and didn't smile back. He just followed us as Vince helped me up the stairs and into my bedroom, and I guess Riley followed us, too.

In my room I said, "Ta da!" because it is kind of a nice room, with all the French posters and everything.

Vince picked up a French dictionary that was on my desk and said "Voulez-vous coucher avec moi, ce soir?"

"That is so lame. That's the sentence everybody knows—"

I didn't get to finish, because Vince was kissing me and pushing me back onto the bed, and I was trying to push him away, thinking how I didn't want Matt to think I liked Vince and not him, and then Matt was there, too, only he was holding my shoulder and helping Vince get my jeans off, and then I realized way too late what was going on.

THE CHAIN AROUND MY NECK

I only remember bits and pieces after that. I think I remember saying, "Please stop. Please," a couple of times, which is when Vince put a hand over my mouth.

The Eiffel Tower had slipped behind me on its chain and that was the thing that made me start to cry—not the way Vince was ripping into me, which was really just the idea of burning pain because I was so numb drunk. Not even his beer breath in my face and his dirty hand clamped so hard over my mouth I knew my lips would be swollen from mashing against my own teeth. It was those hard silver points digging into the top of my spine, and the whole sad idea of how great I'd thought my life was going to be.

When Vince rolled off me, I tried to get up but it was like I had no control over my limbs, and it took hardly anything for him to hold me down with one hand. I heard, "My turn" and "I guess she won't mind," and a lot of laughing, and then Vince practically yelling—"Hey! You gotta use a condom, idiot."

For a minute, I thought they were going to leave me alone because I didn't have any condoms, but they must have brought some because they didn't stop. I kept my eyes clenched tight and there wasn't any point in fighting, and even though no one put a hand over my mouth again, I couldn't do anything but whimper.

I had to open my eyes when I couldn't take the way the room was spinning anymore. It was Matt on top of me, then. His hands were up inside my shirt and I said, "I think I'm going to be sick," but either he didn't hear me or he didn't care, so I just tried to focus on the electric blue letters on the mirror: *Eyes on the prize.*

And, then, Anna was screaming, "Oh my god, what are you doing to her? Get out! Get out, you fucking assholes! I'm calling the police!" And I was afraid they would grab her, too, but she was gone really fast. Then there was just a lot of commotion, the air churning around me like some kind of hurricane and loud voices and everyone scattering like they were getting blown to bits. And then it was quiet, and there was just Anna.

VRYENHOEK

I was still trying to focus and she was saying, "January, it's okay. January? The police are coming. They'll be here soon. Do you want me to call an ambulance?" Her face was really close to mine, close enough that I could see she was crying.

"No, Anna, no. Don't call anybody." I tried to get up, but the room was spinning and I hurt so bad, and I couldn't make my legs move, not at all, so I just had to throw up over the side of the bed. "Just get me some water, okay Anna. That's all."

And she did. She brought me water, and even though she could have just left me there, she went and got a wet towel to clean up the mess I'd made. It was hard to talk because her being so nice was making me cry so much, but I managed to say I was sorry, sorry, sorry for what I'd said to her.

She just whispered, "Shh, it's okay January," and then she sat on the bed and smoothed back my hair, and she didn't even mention the police again until they got there. They talked to me for a long time, while Anna just kind of flapped around quietly behind them.

And later, after I had told them I wasn't going to press charges or anything, when Anna was driving me to the hospital and the sun was coming up, I was thinking how I totally don't get Giselle. Because I would never, ever tell Mom any of this.

EMINENT DOMAIN

MICHELLE BUTLER HALLETT

HOME

A ll I wanted was to help my brother. Even save him—when I got honest with my dreams. First, I have to teach you the language.

Wainscoting. As in, make certain you dust it, or those endlessly hospitable Newfoundland women who employ you out of some demented mix of charity and voyeurism they think is exclusive to them, to their kind culture, will point it out to you and shout the word, as though deafness were part of my being Russian. *The wainscoting, my ducky, bend down now and dust the wainscoting.*

You know what wainscoting is? Do you know change-the-sheets? *Now women here in Newfoundland are a bit more choosy, my ducky. We changes our sheets once a week. I've heard tell about you crowd in Russia, poor, right? One way or another, we has clean sheets once a week. So change the sheets, now. We likes to be clean here in Newfoundland.*

EMINENT DOMAIN

Drains clogged with hair. Towels sour with dirty water. Shaved-off calluses and cut toenails floating in the toilet. Mould on the ceiling. Counters never wiped down. Catshit ground in the pink bath mat. Earwigs in the walls.

Fog. Hovering. Moscow was grey–concrete, teeth, skin. But your fog ...

Psikhushka. Tricky, isn't it? Like a sneeze. Not a sharp and clean word like *Sputnik* or *defector.*

Refugee sounds indecisive.

My older brother, Desya, went to hospital when I was twelve, 1983. We'd been expecting it. Like our father, he'd stumbled into *psikhushka.* Father was not ill. He was nervous. He was Soviet, for God's sake; we were all nervous. My father just couldn't hide it well. In 1978, he was hospitalized with mental illness, for his own protection. Desya and I knew, the same way we knew Americans hated us and Lenin was a reasonable substitute for God, that our father was hospitalized because the old woman who kept watch on our floor, wrote down everyone's coming and going, date and time, had once taught him in school and had once been proven disastrously wrong on a point of history. In truth, our father chuckled, it was the publisher who'd been wrong. Father's textbook was the wrong edition and contained an erroneous photograph. The book looked the same as the others, but there on page fourteen was the photograph with an extra man. The same photograph in the other edition was blurry, like it was defaced with mimetic paint. The pupils laughed; the teacher wept; the principal thrashed Father so badly he was constipated for days: it hurt too much to sit. Father missed a week of school. When he came back, the pupils were quiet and all the books were gone. So was the teacher. The principal taught their class for the rest of the year. Father told Desya and I the story many times, always in a quiet voice, so we'd know better than to question a mere change in photography.

The teacher had gone to the camps, it was said. The word *gulag* was not said.

Father was sickened one day to see her, tiny and balding, in her little chair by the stairwell, her view of the corridor complete. Every flat opened into that corridor. Every day she smiled at Father and nodded, looking up at him from beneath her brow.

Desya's diagnosis had been the same as Father's: sluggishly progressing schizophrenia. Paranoid personality structure. Delusions of a struggle for truth.

Father's photography lesson didn't take. And Desya's hospital was far, far away.

Focus on the future, Desya whispered to me. *Focus on the promise of something else, even if it's late.*

My brother suffered from hope. I just suffered hunger. But I was still young enough not to know any better, and I coddled this demented thought that if I were strong enough to stand in the lines, I'd find Desya's hospital. I did not think he was dead. How could he be? Mother hadn't burnt his pictures as she did Father's.

So when I caught Yuri Tilnokhov studying me as though he had every right beneath his beige overcoat—he did—I clutched at old stories of Tatar princesses and royal consorts and with the bits of memory forced my face to glow. Because in 1988, Yuri Tilnokhov was not a roaming dog cowering at the scent of the alpha, but my personal doorkeeper to files, records, facts and, if I were lucky, truth.

Yuri's eyes were a dull green. His hair was thin and going grey over the ears. He was a listener—surveillance. I was common fruit for him. He could take me any time he pleased.

October 12, 1989; shortly after he pushed a file folder containing information about my brother across his desk. He said it was a winter day, and I'd been standing in line, obscured but not hidden by snow. A winter day standing in line, pick one of thousands—but I said nothing to this listener who offered me gifts, the first one the hardest and the best: a dossier called *Volnokov, Modest (Desya) Pyotorvich.*

Even state-sponsored rations must be paid for.

EMINENT DOMAIN

Yuri smiled, an indulgent uncle with candy. His office—he said it was his office—was white, layered over with brown, and smelled of vinegar, steel and cigarettes. I sat before him in a padded chair, knowing this was to do with Desya, even if it had nothing to do with Desya. Something he'd said, done, someone he'd regarded incorrectly. It was Desya's fault I'd been detained.

Yuri kept nine pencils in a cup. None were sharpened. He knew my full name.

—Serafima Pyotorova Volnokov. Are you and your mother warm enough?

Once, I saw a blurry reproduction of an old map of Russia with paintings of the west and east winds on the edges. Behind Yuri, on the smoke-stained wall, was a map of USSR. The land mass stretched across Europe and Asia like a heavy crown, unsketched hunger and boredom the crown jewels of fear.

Colonel Yuri reached the dossier and turned over the cover. Paperclipped to it: a photo of Desya. Tired, thin. Eyes feverish, face stiff. Hair dirty. Next to that, a typed letter topping many sheets.

Yuri could sing beautifully, low baritone, and he loved giving me bits of *Boris Gudonov* or *Lady Macbeth of Mtsensk*, but when he spoke, he sounded like a tired frog.

—Your brother still needs strong medicines, but he is no longer deteriorating quite so quickly.

Hair fell in my face. The knees of my pants were wrinkly. Pants. I'd caused a fuss, wearing those, Mother finally throwing a plate: *Beg to be thought crazy, then. Beg to be taken away. See if I care!*

Yuri closed the dossier, took it back. —Miss Volnokov, there is something almost electric about you. I saw you standing in line, and the wind tore off your hat. It is the balance of your face, the pride in it.

The floor had been waxed without being stripped. Old wax looked like dirt. Dust and hairs had clumped together where there should have been wainscoting.

—What were you standing in line for?

My face burned. I could not possibly deflect the answer to margarine or soap, because if Colonel Yuri had been watching me, then Colonel Yuri knew. I'd wanted not to keep a bucket soaking rags in the bathroom. I'd wanted to be clean. Or less dirty.

—Menstrual napkins.

Colonel Yuri opened his desk drawer, took out a plain box. Tampons.

I'd seen them on shelves only twice.

He smiled when I took them. —My gift to you, Miss Volnokov.

Another time it was a beige negligee and brown lipstick.

—Fima, you've one gift for me?

No one else called me *Fima*.

I did not come to love Yuri solely because of the gifts. Yuri was both power and hope. With Yuri's favour, I might focus on the promise of something else. I loved him, because through him I could save my brother. If you don't understand that, nothing else matters.

Yuri's hand on my head, pushing me towards his missile, as he called it. My legs got so cold, the negligee was too large, and I left brown lipstick all over him, but for the first time in my life, I felt sexy as a Western woman.

NATIVE

Have you ever deliberately cut yourself? Or bitten your lip 'till it bled? Have you ever run the bath far too hot and forced yourself in, tears cold in comparison? Take some risk to *feel?* Just to slash the inadequate coat you huddled beneath, preferring, quite naturally, a delicate delusion of safety, so long as you met no one's eyes.

Yuri enrolled me in English lessons. Perhaps he had something in mind for me. His importance rose, and soon I was employed, confidential secretary. I don't know how I passed any security check with both Father and Desya hospitalized,

EMINENT DOMAIN

but Yuri said I had talent and might be groomed and ready for when something else came along.

I stayed on Yuri's staff for many years. Twice, he had me service his friends while he watched, but I was so upset, he felt some bare pity and stopped the practice. Meantime, my mother had a warm coat, sufficient food, and one-page reports three times a year on Desya, who had gotten no worse, but no better.

When Yeltsin faced the tanks, I thought Yuri was done—his skill set, as we say, was obsolete. As if oligarchic privatization had no use for listeners and bugs. It hardly mattered; Yuri grumbled, manoeuvred, resigned and soon fell into his wet dream of a frantic trade in so-called state surplus. Weapons, mostly. Free market. Insisted he be called Colonel. Well. The Colonel's missile launches usually aborted. Our international client was a hotter mistress. It was the Chechen names that came to bother me. Yuri said not to think of it. —Clients are clients, Sera. We're just providing the goods.

When the detectives asked me why I was willing to give them lists of the Colonel's Chechen contacts, I said it was because my brother, Desya, died at *Nord-Ost* in 2002. They'd never check. He died shortly beforehand, for me. A bog opened up in Moscow in the late 1990s, sudden exposure of yellowed paper: files. Many, many files. I remember sneezing. I remember transfer reports, lists of drugs, comments on Desya's uncooperative nature, notes on the blessing that followed such behaviour. Subject. In the vein, through the liver, out the urethra. He turned yellow. He turned blue. He died in September of 1990, not even a year after Yuri first spoke to me. All my grey hairs, English phonetics and lipstick from 1989 to 2003, all my telling the mirror I loved him, gone bald and fat and smelling of vinegar, all the semen swallowed—

Focus on the future. Focus on the promise of something else, even if it's late.

I photocopied entire files, carefully at first. Colonel Yuri, the listener, did not bother with cameras.

One day, Yuri took pills to get hard, told me to fax three lists, pay the phone bills, change the passwords, and blow him for old time's sake. I did. Still salty at the mouth, I called one of the detectives and gave him the warning that Yuri was about to flee: *borscht.*

Despite promises of protection, I was beaten about the head and face not far from my flat. It was a white night, all easy to see. My wallet was stolen, just for show. My passport was hidden elsewhere.

I got out. *Unorthodox transport,* the detectives said, *necessity.* More language lessons. Hide in Canada, while the trial was arranged. I was to be congratulated. I had single-handedly toppled Colonel Yuri's weapons trade and caused the arrest of two Chechen arms dealers. Immigration paperwork already in place.

Paperwork gets lost. So do fugitive arms dealers.

LAND

That is how I ended up in the basement of the generally neglected clapboard Methodist Church in Port au Mal. United Church. Not at first—no, first I took a job in a call centre and lived in a basement *apartment,* as you'd call it. Not until I had answered phones and cleaned houses in Newfoundland just over three years did I resort to the church.

Old word: *sanctuary.* Dull phrase: *claim denied.*

My claim wasn't even processed in Newfoundland. No one could explain why the immigration office in St. John's wasn't good enough, why the decision of where to stick the maple leaf up me was made in Moncton.

Little ventilation in the church basement—mould in the walls. Even sprouting across the wainscoting, beautiful little galaxies, spores declaring themselves, unwanted, unseen. Low ceiling, near walls. Try washing yourself at a sink with tiny taps. Try sleeping on a cot in a basement that still smells of white glue, old hymnbooks and hundreds of past fearless children who once sat there for Sunday school. I hate the stink of salt water. I call back to the gulls. Little advocacy group, mostly women who'd once complained I'd been sloppy on the wainscoting. Now they ask me, nearly sincere: *How are you doing, my love?*

Of course I want to stay.

Of course my life is in danger. That is not enough. Truth to the rumours I was connected with organized crime and therefore undesirable? The detectives I worked with might answer that, but they are not to be found. So long as I stay in the basement of the church, Canada cannot deport me.

I loved my brother.

Focus on the future. Focus on the promise of something else.

All I see is distance.

A HOLE FULL OF NOTHING

STEVE VERNON

1

This is how it all went down. Tommy said it was a good deal, and I guess he ought to know what he's talking about. Street fighting, he said. It's big money, he said. All we've got to do is to burn ourselves a few DVD copies and sell them.

So what do you know about burning, I asked. The last time I looked, you needed to read the instructions on a box of strike-anywhere matches.

It's easy, he told me. I've got it all figured out.

Whenever Tommy tells me he's got things all figured out, I start to worry.

Or, at least, I ought to.

So, who's going to fight, I asked.

You, for one, he said. You're the fighter, aren't you?

I was afraid he'd say that. People had been telling me I was a fighter ever since that asshole with the braces.

It's a good idea, Tommy said. We're going to make us some money.

45

A HOLE FULL OF NOTHING

He keeps saying that word, money, like the ka-ching of a cash register is going to talk me into it.

Too damn bad for me that he's probably right.

Tommy's always right. I think when he gets older, he ought to run for prime minister or something higher. Marked for greatness, that's what my dad would say. Well, actually, my dad used to say that Tommy was a walking piece of something that had probably crawled from out of the wrong hole in his momma's gearbox and maybe he ought to crawl on back and simmer a little while longer until he's cooked all the way through. Since then, my Dad's opinion of Tommy has slid a little downhill and puddled around his ankles like a pair of worn out boxer shorts. Gravity worked, I guess, even though my dad didn't anymore.

I told Tommy what my dad said, but Tommy only said that my dad ought to watch out for what he said or else he'd learn a lesson from his betters. I'm not sure which betters Tommy was talking about, and Tommy never got around to elaborating upon that threat. Anyway, my dad is still talking and I'm still waiting for Tommy to teach dad a thing or two, like maybe how to clean Tommy's blood from off of my dad's knuckles if Tommy ever works up the nerve to try.

He won't. Tommy's not a fighter. I'm the fighter. Everybody at school knows that. Tommy's a talker and a dreamer. That's different from being a fighter. A fighter goes and gets what he wants, while a talker just stands around and tries to talk somebody else into getting it for him.

I'll show them all, Tommy said. I'm going to make myself a mark.

Yeah right, is what I think, but I don't say it out loud so as not to hurt Tommy's feelings. You don't hurt your friend's feelings, not if you wanted to keep them feeling friendly. That was tricky with Tommy. With Tommy, there were two kinds of people: him and them. As far as Tommy was concerned, the whole world was trying to gang up on him and his only chance was to screw them first.

VERNON

I didn't think like that. Not much, anyways. Besides, Tommy never followed through on any of his threats or honoured any of his promises. Tommy was way too busy dreaming. He always had one kind of a plan or another cooking on the back burner.

Last year, he was going to make a fortune stealing wire and stripping it down to sell to the scrap metal dealer. Tommy made about seven bucks before shorting out the town's power supply and damn near electrocuting himself in the process. He charred off his fingerprints, and I think that was the only thing that kept him from getting caught.

This year, it was fighting.

It's like that Ultimate Fighting, Tommy said. Folks will pay a lot to see that sort of shit on DVD.

Folks like who? I asked.

Folks like everybody, Tommy said. Everybody around here from Yarmouth to Shelburne is bound to want to own a copy and watch it. What else is there to watch around here? The ocean?

He had a point. This far out in the boonies even tired old Yarmouth seemed exciting. Where we lived, there was nothing much to do but stare at the waves running in and out, always reaching and never quite getting, and that got old pretty fast.

I threw a rock out into the water. It made a splash and a gulp sound like a bullfrog hop. The rock made a hole in the water, sank straight down and the hole filled in. If the whole process had a deeper meaning, I don't know what it was. It just passed the time, is all.

Passing time passes for fun and excitement here in the unwiped asshole of lower Nova Scotia. The town has got a name, but nobody ever uses it. Who needs a name in a dump like this? A rose by any other name still stank of the horseshit you planted it in. About the only thing to do around here is drive through and there isn't much of that going on since they up and moved the highway.

A HOLE FULL OF NOTHING

They passed us by, my dad would rant. Cut us off and passed us by, hoping we'd rot away like a tied off leg.

Right, Dad. Ottawa itself has declared war on this little craphole of a town.

Tommy kept on talking. We'll make some money, he said for the fifteenth time. We'll make our mark. People will be talking about us all over Nova Scotia. Hell, they'll be talking all across Canada.

You sure about that Tommy? I asked.

Sure, I'm sure. People love mixed martial arts.

The way he said it sounded like a mixed drink or maybe mixed nuts, and I wondered if Tommy really knew what he was talking about.

Name somebody, I said.

Lots of people like it. They like it because it's so different all of the time. You've got your wrestling and your jujitsu and your tae-kwan-do. It's like an all-you-can-eat pizza buffet.

Right, I said. All the pizza you can eat. That's some kind of variety you're talking about.

Tommy doesn't appreciate sarcasm much. He glared at me like my IQ-ometer had fallen by about sixty-eight degrees.

Don't you ever watch Spike television? he asked.

Now, Tommy knew damn well my family couldn't afford cable television, not since the fish plant shut down. Dad used to bring home pretty good money when he worked there, but nowadays he just sits at the kitchen table sipping on a luked-over cup of tea. I think the luked-over tea started as a way to save on tea bags, but the whole thing had become a kind of a habit and a ritual for my dad. He'd get about fifteen cups a day out of a single tea bag, just refilling the cup over and over onto the sogged out tea bag.

And while he sipped, he'd rant. My dad was a champion class ranter. I think he practised ranting in the garage when nobody was listening. It was kind of like he was warming up for something, like shadow-boxing with his mouth, only I never really have figured out just what Dad was getting ready for. Some war that had never been declared, I guess.

VERNON

The fish are still out there, Dad would say, but the goddamn government won't let us fish them. They let those foreign factory ships gut the sea clean clear empty while hardworking fishermen sit on the docks, fartless and broke.

That's about all that Dad does these days, sipping tea and staring down towards the harbour and cursing the goddamn factory ships. I don't even know if there are any factory ships out there, but the way that Dad talks they must look something like Darth Vader's Death Star and they're manned by zombie mutant gerbils and they must be about as toxic as the bubonic plague.

About the only other thing my dad does these days is go out to the Seven-Eleven to buy himself some smokes and scratch-and-win tickets.

That and the tea, which Dad never did learn to like.

A man can't even afford himself a decent drink these days, Dad complained. No beer, no rum and no whiskey. Nothing but lukewarm piss-thin tea, day after goddamn day, you talk about living shit-poor in a damn hard old spot.

Talking with my dad does wonders for my vocabulary. No wonder I failed English last year. I don't get it. It was that last essay that did it. I figure I don't know what that teacher was so pissed about. Fuck's a word, isn't it? Anyway, what are they doing teaching English in our schools? We live in Canada, don't we? We ought to be learning to speak Canadian.

I already know all I need to know about speaking Nova Scotian. I didn't need to go to school for that. There's a rhythm to speaking Nova Scotian, that's got a little of the ebb tide and the mud flats and that feeling that you get when your best girl tells you that she just wants to be friends. Nova Scotian words are mostly spelled out in multiples of four letters and when it came to four letter words, my Dad was a mathematical wizard.

Why don't you go look for a job? dad asked me the other day. We could sure use the money.

Why don't you go look for one yourself, was what I thought, but I knew better than to say it out loud.

A HOLE FULL OF NOTHING

That's my plan, I said.

I did have myself a plan, you understand. I figured I would get myself into trade school and maybe become a plumber or an electrician. I had heard that both of these professions paid pretty damn well and that kind of appealed to my way of thinking.

I've got to finish high school first, I said to Dad. Then maybe go to trade school and make something out of myself.

Dad snorted like he was trying to back-swallow a head cold. Trade school takes money, he said, and you don't have any.

He had a point.

Okay Dad, so maybe you're right. So maybe I've been looking for work on the internet.

He cocked his eyebrow at me, raising it high and arched like a woolly caterpillar rainbow.

As far as I can tell, there's nothing but a whole lot of nothing on the internet, Dad said. Mind you, my dad still thinks that websites are places where spiders hang their hats.

So what do you know about the internet? I asked.

I know what I need to goddamn know, he said. I looked on the internet once and I couldn't find anything more than a load of women taking their bikinis off. I looked for hours, he said. I wasted a whole morning.

I bet he did. It takes a lot of time to run a keyboard one-handed.

There are a ton of jobs on the internet, I said. You just have to look is all. I knew one guy he got himself a good government job just by looking on the internet.

A good job, eh? So what's he do?

He looks on the internet, I said. He's a researcher.

I made that whole story up about looking for work on the internet and Dad knows it but he sure can't prove it. I don't imagine he'll even try. The best he can do is just sit there at the kitchen table, hunched down over his scratch-and-win tickets, scratching off the rows of spaces with the edge of a penny. His knuckles are as white as a nun's left ass cheek from squeezing that penny so hard. The dust from the scratch tickets piled up on the table top and worked into his fingers. It went nicely with the nicotine stains tattooed on his knuckles and the tea mug haloes etched on the table top.

Where's Mom? I asked.

Bingo, Dad said.

Throwing money away is what I think but all I asked Dad was—did she win yet?

She won last month, Dad said, like he's proud of her. Her shining moment, winning two hundred dollars, not bad for a night's work.

Actually, she won the money two months ago. And those two hundred dollars were spent by last month, on this month's Bingo cards. I might be flunking English but I can still do the math better than Dad can. My dad doesn't think numbers count for all that much. In fact, my dad's mental calendar has been running a little slow lately. He blames it on living here in the Maritimes.

Forget about your daylight savings time, Dad always tells me, here in the Maritimes time is an endangered fossil fuel—slow, creeping and hard to find. Living here has given me a case of the all-the-timers disease.

That's Alzheimer's, Dad.

We've got an aunt who has Alzheimer's, so I know all about it. Once a month, Mom drags us up to see her and, most times, she doesn't know us any more than I know the pope. The idea of Alzheimer's kind of scares me. It's a little like having your eye knocked back into yourself so that all you can stare at is your own personal TV reruns.

No sir, Dad corrected me, it's maritimers all-the-timers. It's a condition that you get from sitting around with nothing to do and no cash and all of the time in the world to spend it on.

He does have a point.

Maybe you're right, Dad. Maybe I ought to head for the Prairies. I bet I'll find something out west.

There's no call for moving, he said.

A HOLE FULL OF NOTHING

I expected that. Whenever Dad thinks about moving, he grows anchors and mud banks.

Lots of people move, I said.

Not our family, he said. We stick where God plunked us, close to home. Your family has lived here in Nova Scotia since the first tide turned.

Then he pointed his finger up the hill towards the town graveyard and I know what's coming. I've heard the granddad rant maybe sixty or a hundred times this year. My dad is like a CD set on random play, with only so many tracks and only so many rants to go around. He just keeps flipping the channels from rant to rant, clicking through them daily, as if he wants to be sure he doesn't miss any.

Your granddad is buried in that graveyard, Dad said.

He's not really. Granddad died at sea in a storm that carried his body out into open water. There's nothing up there in that graveyard but an empty coffin ballasted in with a baker's dozen beach stones.

I've got to go, I said. Maybe look for a job.

Pick me up a pack of cigarettes while you're at it, my dad said.

Pick them up yourself, I said, before I could think better of it.

Dad up and cracked me one on the cheek, right hard.

Mind your lip, chummy, he said.

I nodded, not saying anything more. I backed out of the door, in case he's feeling ambitious enough to take another swing at me. I rubbed at the cheek where it smarted. The mark will have faded before I reached the street. If it doesn't, I'll blame it on the chill morning wind.

And pick me up those smokes, Dad shouted as I headed down the sidewalk. It's the liveliest I've seen him in months. Then he slammed the door and went back inside to those goddamn scratch-and-wins that never would.

Which brings me back to Tommy, whom I run into after running right out of my house.

So what do you think about street fighting? Tommy asked.

I rubbed my cheek, wondering if it was bruised over or faded clean. Dad would be wild if he heard what Tommy and me were up to.

Sure, I said. Count me in.

2

Sometimes I get so angry, I want to hit something. I used to pound my fist into my pillow before I went to sleep. I hit the wall once and broke the plaster. I covered it up with a poster of some rapper. I take the poster down at night and stare at the hole behind it. The hole looks a little like a mouth getting set to eat me.

I hope it does.

Alright, so I know that sounds kind of foolish, but you have to understand that this was about two or two-thirty in the morning. The time of night when the clock radio glows like that asshole with the braces back in grade three who used to steal my toque and blow his nose on it and throw it up into the pine tree out back of the school.

We used to call that tree the toque tree because there were so many winter hats hung up in there, and that asshole hung most of them. And that same asshole was sitting in my bedroom at two or two-thirty in the morning staring at me and grinning through his neon green clock radio braces.

I swung on him one day and corked him a hard one and he fell on me like a tree and I remember the teacher pulling me up and my shirt was wet and I could taste gravel, only it wasn't gravel and the kid had a crooked funny kind of smile from where I'd bent his braces, and ever since then, people said I was a fighter and then one night at two or two-thirty in the morning, I put my fist through the wall thinking that it was that asshole with the braces and Dad never woke up.

Some nights I peeled that rap poster down, unsticking the Scotch tape an ick at a time, until the wall was bare. I don't know who the rapper was. I stole the poster from off of a locker at school. He's probably got a name something like Big Rappy Jayhay or Five Knuckles 'Mo. All of those rappers have the same kind of cool names, different, so they stand out.

Maybe I'll change my name one day to something like Throwmaster Smackdown. That'd put the fear into anyone who heard it.

Some nights I just lay there and whispered words into the broken-holed mouth in the wall. It's too late to make sense, I just kept whispering and hoped that the words would pile up like snow into some kind of sense, but they never did.

It beats the hell out of dreaming, which I don't any more. Nowadays, all my dreams sound like static on the radio, blizzards in March, with the snow rattling against the window pane and the wind whistling down the flue hole.

3

I figured I'd better train for the fight, so I watched every Rocky movie up to number five, because that's how many were in the set that Tommy five-finger-jacked for me at the shopping mall. We were watching the one where Rocky runs up the mountain and shouts the Russian guy's name. I can't remember which number it was.

Tommy was sitting beside me, dreaming out loud as usual.

We're going to be rich, Tommy said.

So, what are you going to do with all the money you make from selling the DVDs?, I asked Tommy.

We make, he corrected me. We're going to make the money, not just me. We're a team, we are.

Yeah, whatever, I said, not bothering to correct him.

You see, that's the difference between Tommy and me. I've never really believed in Tommy's dreams and schemes. They're just a way for me to pass the time is all. Tommy buys into his own imagination, but I keep my feet planted in the dirt.

I want to use the money to save and send my girlfriend Shelley to Canadian Idol next year, Tommy said. She can really sing. You've heard her.

VERNON

I knew what she sounded like. She used to be my girlfriend, only one day I walked in on her and Tommy banging each other like a pair of drums. I stood there with that sort of smile on my face that people wear when they don't know what in the hell else they should say. Then I swallowed that smile and said that everything was fine. I never did really care for Shelley that much at all. She was always too afraid to swallow.

I had heard Shelley sing and she sounded like a bagpipe stuffed full of barn cats in heat, only not so pretty. Besides which she was going to leave Tommy sooner or later because everybody knew that she was already banging five other guys.

Like I said, Tommy was a bit of a dreamer. He couldn't deal with reality the way I could.

So you figure you're ready for the fight? Tommy asked.

I touched the cheek ruefully. I still hadn't told Dad about the fighting. He'd be wild if he'd heard what I was up to. He'd be absolutely pissed.

Yeah, I tell Tommy. I'm ready.

We stopped watching the Rocky movies because one of them had a scratch in the disc and it kept showing the same scene over and over. Him drinking eggs, gulping them down, over and over, while the music kept pounding louder and louder.

I tried drinking eggs once and puked them all out.

I guess I was too chicken to swallow.

4

We spent a week digging the arena.

At least, arena was what we called it on Monday. On Tuesday, we called it the hole, on Wednesday, that godforsaken shitdig, on Thursday, a pain in the ass, on Friday, we called it a well to hell, but on Saturday, we called it the pit. Actually, Saturday was the first time that the pit really began to look like maybe we knew what we were doing.

This is really a cool pit, Tommy decided. He was wearing a big cowboy hat, like John Wayne, only it didn't look like it fit him. I'd never seen him wear a cowboy hat before today. It didn't really suit him much, but I didn't figure on telling him that. Maybe he just figured it was tick season and he'd be better off wearing a big old hat.

Tommy had brought two new buddies with him to help. Hank Drummond and Lorne Smith. They were there for the muscle and the fighting. Hank was all muscle, tough and lean with a little Mi'kmaq in him, although his mother swore he was pure Nova Scotian. He wore a big old hoop earring fish hooked through one eyebrow. I wondered what that felt like going in and decided I never really wanted to find out.

Lorne was the bigger of the two, but not in a good way. He had run to fat and caught it, big time. All soft and mushy around the middle. He had a mean streak in him that only came out around people smaller than him, which was mostly everybody but Hank and Tommy. He was bigger than both of them combined, but somehow they both seemed to stand a little taller than Lorne did.

If I had to fight either of them, I hoped it would be Lorne. I figured I could take Lorne, if I got lucky. Lorne was big but slow and no kind of a real fighter. He just came at you like a bulldozer. You could wear him down if you were fast enough. An army of roadrunning comets couldn't have worn down Hank. Hank was hard, tough and mean.

We ought to have a cage, I said. All of these tournaments are usually fought in a cage.

No, Tommy said, a pit will do. He'd seen folks fighting in a pit in a movie or maybe a comic book. I don't know which but it had taken him over like some kind of an inspired vision.

All of the big fights are in metal cages, I repeated.

Yeah, Hank said. He's right, they are.

Tommy wasn't listening. Tommy was really good at not listening. There were times when you would swear his ears were nothing but stone jug handles hooked on either side of his head.

So, why haven't we got a cage? I asked.

We've got this pit, Tommy said. It's just as good.

VERNON

We dug the pit out in the woods. Three of us were digging and Tommy was doing most of the talking and pointing. I wondered if talking and pointing was any harder than digging. It was damn hard work digging. There was nothing but rocks and roots and dirt. It was probably the hardest I'd ever worked at anything before in my life. It kind of felt good to see it done, to look down into that hole I'd dug and say to myself—there, I did that.

And now, I was thinking about the cage.

How do you guys like my hat? Tommy asked.

It makes good shade, I said, trying hard to stay diplomatic.

I found it at the Frenchy's, Tommy said. I figure we can draw names from the hat to decide who fights who.

I kept seeing the cage rising up from the walls of the pit, looking like something out of a science fiction movie. It would be so damn cool.

So who's doing the fighting? I asked.

So far, I figure you three, Tommy said. Lorne's big and Hank is tough and you're the fighter. At least everybody says you are.

I knew that he was just trying to stir me up, so I paid him no attention and kept talking about what I wanted him to hear.

That's not much of a stable to work from, I said. We ought to have a cage.

I wasn't letting that go. I had a vision, and I had to see it come true.

A stable, Hank said. Are we going to be riding horses while we fight?

I've been doing some research on the internet, using the Google and such, I said. I had found out that's what they call a gang of fighters. A stable.

Well, maybe we can fight two or three times, Lorne said. We could wear masks, like in the wrestling.

I looked at Lorne. He wasn't helping much. Besides, as big as he was, there wasn't anyone in town wouldn't recognize him, no matter what sort of a mask he wore.

A HOLE FULL OF NOTHING

Have we got a video camera yet? I asked Tommy.

No, not yet, Tommy said, but we've got ourselves a hat.

At least we've got a pot to piss in, if nothing else happens, Hank said.

And that's when that idea pushed up out of the dirt of my imagination and I went and said it.

I said, I know where we can find the bars for the cage.

5

We hit the plumber's shed on Sunday night. Breaking into his place was pretty easy. Lorne took a hammer to the padlock, and it came off on the second swing. I kept expecting alarm bells to go off and guard dogs to start barking but who was I kidding? This was the lower asshole of Nova Scotia we were looking at, not anywhere handy to New York or Toronto. Security measures were at a bare minimum.

Get in there, Tommy said. It was your idea.

It was my idea, and I was damn proud of it.

So, I stepped in first. I guess it only made sense. If there were any trouble, I needed to be the one to face it. I was the fighter, after all. I was the one best equipped to handle anything we ran into.

Besides, I had thought of the idea first.

I stepped out into the darkness feeling a little as if I were stepping off into the Grand Canyon, blindfolded. It gets pretty damn dark out here in the country, and it's even darker way back in the back ass of a plumber's shed. What made things worse was the ski mask I was wearing, which kept on getting in my eyes. I had bought the ski mask at Frenchy's in case we needed it to fight in but I figured if we were going to become burglars, it sure wouldn't hurt. Besides, it beat the hell out of Tommy's damn cowboy hat.

Lorne had brought along a pickup truck that he'd probably stolen and he backed it up to the shed. That truck sure was loud and the exhaust damn near smoked us out the plumbing shed. I was sure we'd die from the fumes or else we'd wake up the whole town with the truck's revving engine and the sound of our wheezing hacking coughs.

We filled the back end of the truck with as much ABS pipe as we could find. I figured it would be a lot easier to work with than copper piping. All I needed now was some glue and a hacksaw.

We found both of those on the plumber's workbench.

I stood there for a long time staring at the work bench. I wondered how it would be to own a workbench like this and call myself a plumber. It couldn't be harder than calling myself a fighter, I figured. Besides, it didn't look all that much different from my dad's workbench.

I wanted to leave the plumber an IOU note but I figured the police might be able to use that as evidence. I told myself that once we'd made our money selling the fight DVDs, we could pay the plumber back for his missing supplies.

You see, I had already begun to believe in Tommy's big plan.

6

I spent the rest of the night building the cage, cutting the pipe and gluing them together. I was proud of myself by the end of it. I used full lengths of ABS as bars and Lorne and Hank took turns driving them into the dirt at the bottom of the pit with a sledgehammer. Then, I used ABS T-joints and shorter pieces of pipe to join the bars together at the top.

The glue and lack of sleep was getting to me. I wasn't seeing any flying codfish or pink whales, you understand, but everything seemed clearer and louder to me, as if I was in touch with some sort of a deeper power.

We've got to keep this a secret, I said to Tommy. We could get in a lot of trouble if they catch us.

No kidding, Captain Obvious, Lorne said. Why don't you tell us something we don't know?

I was talking about stealing the pipes, but Tommy and Lorne thought I was talking about the fight itself. Hank didn't appear to care one bit one way or the other. Maybe that was what it took to be as tough as Hank was. You had to not care what happened or what went on. You had to grow yourself a set of horse blinders and look straight on at what ever it was you were headed towards.

We can't keep this secret, Tommy said. We need people to know about the fight. How else are we going to make any money?

I stared at Tommy, wondering what in the hell I was thinking about. He was still wearing that damn cowboy hat. I think he was beginning to enjoy wearing it.

This fighting isn't against the law is it? I asked.

Of course it isn't, Tommy said. They don't arrest you for fighting.

You've looked into this, I said, trying hard to hide the question mark that was hidden inside my statement.

Sure I have looked into it, Tommy said indignantly. We're going to make a lot of money. This is a great idea.

There he goes on about the money again.

So when do we tell people about the fight? I asked.

Tommy smiled at that. He really looked proud of himself. I think this was his big shining moment.

My dad used to tell me that every man in the world should look forward to his one big shining moment. There's a time when we all get to climb just as high as we are able to, he said, and when we're up there, we ought to make the most of it.

And then he went back to scratching his goddamn scratch-and-win tickets.

I've already taken care of that, Tommy said. I've set up a site on MySpace and we've had hundreds of hits so far.

Yeah, I said, thinking about a very different kind of hit. I was wondering just how many hundred were in a hundreds and how hard hundreds of hits could hurt.

This is a good cage, Tommy said, grinning at me like he meant it.

I grinned back in amazement. I think that was the first compliment Tommy ever gave me. It sure was the best.

Thanks, I said.

VERNON

The fight's tomorrow night, Tommy said. You better get home and get some sleep.

I stood there in the pit, staring out through the bars I'd built, grinning and stoned on ABS glue and about three hundred and sixty eight hours without sleep.

This is going to be great, I said.

7

I spent the night in bed. When I woke up, that rap poster had fallen off of the wall and that empty fist hole was talking to me. Or maybe I had taken the poster down again and couldn't remember. I was still pretty wasted from the night before. I lay there under the covers, listening to what the fist hole was saying, only it seemed to me like it was speaking in Swahili because I couldn't understand a word it was telling me.

I leaned my ear against it.

I could hear the sound of the waves from down on the shore and it felt as if that sound might have been coming from out of the mouth of my wall's fist hole. It made a hollow sound that whispered about deepness that I couldn't imagine, anchors pulling down and chains and chests and dead men's coffins and a whole lot of cold wet darkness.

I closed my eyes.

Wake up man.

I opened my eyes.

It was Tommy. Standing there over me like he'd just tucked me into bed. I didn't ask how he'd got into my bedroom.

We've got to go, he said.

8

They drove me to the fight in Lorne's pickup truck. We all smoked some weed while we were driving and Tommy gave me some sort of a pill.

Take this, he told me.

By this point in time, I'd given up on free choice and had decided to do whatever Tommy told me to do. I swallowed the

A HOLE FULL OF NOTHING

pill down without a word of protest. Tommy seemed as good a compass as any to follow right now. The fact was I was still trying to wake myself up, while everybody else in the truck seemed to be seriously determined to get themselves good and stupid.

And there were a lot of people on that truck. Tommy and Lorne and me jammed into the cab, with maybe twenty people wedged into the truck bed.

That's our audience, Tommy shouted at me over the music that was blaring on the truck radio. Only his mouth was moving one way and the words were coming out another and underneath his words I could hear that sound of the wall's fist hole rising up over the radio music.

Have they all paid to see me fight? I asked. That was pretty impressive, that many people turning out to just to see a few Nova Scotia boys throw down on each other. I felt about ten feet tall, which was a pretty good trick given as how I was currently jammed beneath the sweaty fat folds of Lorne's right armpit and Tommy's bony shoulder bones.

Tommy looked over at me like I was the number one depositor in the Bank of Stupid and I shrank down about two or three feet.

They're just the audience, Tommy said. I've invited them along. Some of them will buy copies of the film we make.

So we've got a camera? I asked.

I've got it worked out, Tommy said. Here, have another pill.

I took it, and for a while, things began to blur.

9

I woke up sleeping under a jack pine. The wind was making a whispering sound through the dead brown needles that had been burnt by the summer heat and the acid rain. I could hear people yelling and it sounded as if they were years away.

Wake up, Tommy said. It's time for you to fight.

I tried to stand up, but my legs were made from rubber and Slinky toys. I felt itchy, like I was covered in mosquito bites and my mouth felt dry and numb at the same time and the world was turning slowly.

Come on, said Tommy. Don't keep everybody waiting.

I shook it off and cowboyed up. This is what I said I'd do and I wasn't about to wuss out now.

Snap to it, Tommy said. Get your ass into that cage.

I could see it now and it looked pretty freaking cool. That big old cage, all black under the moonlight with all of those people standing around it. I could see the print of the ABS labels on the pipe standing out in the darkness. A part of me wanted to stop the fight and paint over the lettering with some black paint but there was no time to stop.

Do we have a camera? I asked. Where's the camera?

Shelley brought her cell phone, Tommy said. She can shoot movies on it.

I could see her now, standing close to the bars of the cage with her cell phone camera up and ready. I wondered just how good of a picture it would shoot here in the dark and I wondered if maybe we should have set this whole thing up in the daytime and then I decided it didn't really matter.

I was here to fight and that's all that counted right now.

I climbed down into the pit. It seemed darker and deeper by moonlight. Tommy still hadn't told me just who I had to fight.

Hey, a voice said from out of the darkness.

Oh shit.

It was Hank.

He was standing there in the center of the pit, waiting for me. He had the big old pirate earring that he wore fish-hooked into his eyebrow and he had war painted his face up with his mother's lipstick. I didn't know that Mi'kmaq wore war paint and maybe Hank didn't either. Maybe he just saw it on television. The war paint should have looked silly but in the darkness and the closeness of the pit, it scared the hell out of me.

He stepped up almost lazily taking a swing that clipped me on the side of the ear and left it numb. I took two steps back but he hadn't been trying to hurt me so much as make me take those two steps back. While I was stepping back, Hank stepped up and brought his knee into my ribs and I thought I felt something break.

Holy shit.

I came around trying to swing on him and he sort of leaned back with my swing and blocked me at the wrist. He blocked me hard and it felt as if the bones in my wrist were ringing like a recess bell, only Hank wasn't giving me any time out. He brought his arm up short and sharp, getting his hip behind it, and tagged me on the nose. I felt a water balloon swell up inside my nostrils, and when it broke, my face felt warm and wet all over.

I could hear the crowd above us roaring and yelling and I knew that some of them were watching the fight and some of them were just standing around and shooting the shit with each other. This really wasn't much of a big deal to them, no matter what Tommy said. They could see this sort of thing on the television and the pay per view and at the DVD store any time they wanted to.

I jacked my arm forward, catching Hank in his gut, but his abs felt as if he cranked out about ten thousand crunches every morning before eating a breakfast of washboards and corrugate iron. He brought his head down into a nasty hard head butt that broke a sunrise under my vision and damn brought sunset down on after it.

We were in close now and I forked my hands up wildly, catching hold of his T-shirt collar and trying to choke him but strangulation is a hell of a lot harder than it looks on television.

Hank hammered his fist into my cheek again and again and I knew it was probably hurting him nearly as bad as it was hurting me but that didn't matter one bit right now.

I grabbed at his face and I felt my finger poke into the pirate earring and I yanked it out just as hard as I could. I felt it tear, his eyebrow giving way, and I could see the blood washing down his face over his red lipstick war paint. The forehead bleeds really easily and Hank's head looked like a giant angry raspberry.

I stood there for what seemed to be a hundred minutes or so, staring up at the eyebrow ring in my hand. I could see the moon peeking down through the hole in the earring like a head in a sniper scope and I wondered if this was what Frodo felt like on the edge of Mount Doom and then Hank fell on me and avalanched a half a dozen more hard slamming jackhammers to my face.

I jerked my knee up just as hard as I could and caught him under the chin and his teeth and jaw bone made a clacking sound and I thought I saw that twisted brace grin of that toque-chucking asshole back in grade three, whose smile never really grew back and I thought I saw Shelley staring down at me through her cell phone camera and I wondered if she was trying to make some kind of a crazy telephone call to me from outer space and then I brought my elbow down just as hard as I could about five or six times into the top of Hank's skull and something broke.

The next thing I knew, I was standing over Hank and he was laying there in the dirt and I wasn't sure if he was ever going to grow back straight and I could hear that hushed seashell roar of my wall's fist hole shouting over everything and Tommy was down there beside me holding my fist up in the air.

That's going to leave a mark, he said.

I wasn't sure if Tommy was talking about Hank or me but it didn't matter much right now. I grinned as hard I could through broken teeth, enjoying my shining moment, while I could.

Five minutes later, Shelley used her cell phone to dial 911 because Hank wasn't breathing right and his eyes were all funny and blood was coming out of his nostrils and ears, and I stood there listening to the sound of the wind whistling through the pine needles and the distant waves beating against the rocks and Hank's funny breathing. I kept thinking about

A HOLE FULL OF NOTHING

that film Shelley had shot on her camera and all of these spectators who had been watching the whole thing and me, here in this pit, staring out through these bars with this bloodstained earring clenched in my fist, wondering what came next.

NIGHT DIVIDES THE DAY

LEE D. THOMPSON

Jade wouldn't stop laughing. We were in an open field, and nothing was familiar. The stars had slipped behind night-grey clouds, and only our silhouettes were visible.

We are so lost, one of us said.

And I was laughing too. Where the fuck are we? I said. Jade gasped, grabbed my arm and pulled me to the ground. Look, she said. Lie back and look. We lay next to each other and we looked. It's always like that, Derek. We just never see it. Can you imagine if everyone could see it? See how it is? Who would care about anything if we could see it?

I was trying not to laugh.

The grass was wet and long around us, the grass was under my clothing, wrapping my body. Jade's eyes were shining like her teeth, and it was starlight. The grass was her fingers, the grass grew across her navel and her panties, with red and white stripes, were stretched between her knees.

We weren't even on the grass, but in the air, and there was ocean between the air and the grass.

NIGHT DIVIDES THE DAY

Jade gasped.
I love you, Jade.

Hours later, during the ride home, leaning over the back of the pickup and puking my guts clean, I began to cry. There were wild orchids along the side of the road, sprouting from the forest, and though it was early, you knew the day was going to be a scorcher. I don't know why the crying began then.

Case appeared to be asleep. Tyler was staring at the tops of passing trees, or at the climbing sun flashing in between. J.P. and Serge lay side by side, smoking, talking.

The pickup jolted over pot holes, kicked out gravel and raced over narrow bridges and blind hills. Houses that seemed asleep the night before, it was obvious now that they'd been abandoned for decades. Last night, I thought Jade was crazy when she pleaded for us to stop the truck, to party there instead. "It'll be a blast, guys," she said. "I have five hits of acid and some E. *Come on, you fuckers...*"

And Case said, "There's no beer there, Jade—the beer's at the cabin."

"Well let's get the beer and come back. Come *on...*"

Which abandoned house had she pointed to? I thought she had wanted to show up at some strangers' place, break in, but had I known the house was deserted, I would have jumped out then and said yeah, you fuckers, go get your beer, Jade and I will party alone. If she'd wanted to jump off a bridge and drown, just because it would've been fun, I would have done that too.

"Will you sit back down?" Ty said. "You're making me nervous leaning out like that." Tyler, I wanted to say, you don't know what happened last night.

I sat next to Tyler, back to the cab window, head between my knees.

"Just don't puke again," he said.

"Ty, it doesn't make sense. Why would she...?"

Tyler pulled his cap over his eyes and crossed his arms. He stretched his legs out and sighed. Serge and J.P. continued to talk, butt their smokes on the box's rusted floor. And Case, I knew he wasn't sleeping. I wondered if he would sleep at all this week.

The pickup turned sharply, entered a covered bridge and I closed my eyes. My head was pounding and my body felt dry as twine. Last night, while cutting through the same covered bridge, on the way to the cabin, Jade and I had screamed at the top of our lungs. She was trying to get us all to scream in unison. "Derek will," she said. "Derek's not a lame-ass like you guys, right, Derek?" She held my hand and the bridge passed over and blotted out the stars.

I remember Case watching us, looking annoyed. "He hates it when I'm like this," Jade whispered. She grabbed my head and put her lips to my ear. "Hey," she said, "have you ever done acid? In the woods, it's the best place. The stars are awesome." I nodded. I wondered how jealous Case would be. Ty had told me Jade and Case were no longer dating, but said they were still fucking.

In school, she was the girl who was almost never there. I'd see her a few times a month, in math class, bored, sometimes hung over. She had a way of sitting and tilting her head, gazing at the floor. Her limbs were long. It was hard to keep my eyes off her. Everyone said she was messed up and it made you think of wild nights, of sex and drugs. High school vice has little variation.

Once she'd asked me for a cigarette, and another time asked if we'd had a test the day before. I told her she was lucky, it was only tomorrow. Thanks, she said. Of course, she wasn't in class the next day. Roll call and no response, the teacher would just move on, unconcerned, next name. Jade's not here, I wanted to say. Do you want me to go find her?

She's sexy as hell, I agree, Ty had said, but Christ, get over it, Derek. She's totally fucked up and a little out your league. That family of hers? Stay away. She's hardcore, man, and you? You've been drunk, what, twice you said?

I told him maybe three times.

NIGHT DIVIDES THE DAY

Smoked pot?

Makes me cough.

Just give it up. You're going to really embarrass yourself one day, you know? And, if you do, I'm gone. We are not friends anymore.

I think she needs good friends, Ty, someone she can trust.

Ty laughed. You totally want to bone her.

Then, two weeks ago Ty calls me, says, Guess who I was partying with last night? I heard the words Casey English. Don't worry, he said, I didn't tell him anything. And yes, Derek, Jade was there. Fuck off, I said, and Ty laughed, said Hey, do you know what her real name is? It ain't Jade, that's for sure. It's Janice.

No way.

Yeah, but everyone called her J., then it became Jade because, you know, Jay's a guy's name.

Janice?

And then, two days ago, Ty comes by and says, Friday night, there's going to be a party out in Hillsdale. Too bad you're not invited. I can imagine you there, standing in a corner staring at her all night. I told him I wouldn't go anyways and he called me a pussy and next thing I knew, I was going no matter what. Ty's funny that way.

When the pickup arrived, it was already dark. I squeezed into the back of the cab with Ty and Jade, and Jade greeted me with a whoop and a high five and a hug. She reached into a backpack at her feet and handed me a beer. "Turn it up, fuckers," she called to Corwin, who was driving, and to Case, who was digging through the CDs. *Night divides the day... break on through to the other side.* The truck was humming with it.

"Hey Jade," Ty shouted, "Derek here plays guitar."

Jade's eyes lit, she said it was awesome and said we should start a band. I asked her if she played anything and she said she just wanted to be in a band, she'd do anything, tambourine, or triangle, or—and she scratched her nails on her sneakers—make this sound. "Who cares?" she said. "Everybody's so fucking boring. We'll start a band, OK?"

"OK," I said, nodding.

"What should we call ourselves?" she shouted. "Everybody, let's think of band names."

"The Violet Scrotums," Case shouted.

"I'm fucking serious," Jade said. "A real name, come on."

Outside of town, we stopped and picked up J.P. and Serge, who jumped into the back box. We did the same. Serge, Tyler told me, he could get you anything you want, pot, crystal meth, molly, coke. He's a nice guy, too.

We headed for Hillsdale, the wide river to our left, the suburbs thinning, replaced by farmhouses. Jade was curled in conversation with Serge. Ty slid over and asked me what I thought and all I could say was, wow, she's great. Then Case came over and said, so who the hell are you, man? Case is a big, slow-moving, shaven-headed guy. He kind of ambles along. He loves music, wants to produce it, be the guy behind the sound. I think that's what he and Jade shared, a crazy love of music.

Case had kissed Jade. Case had seen Jade naked, touched her breasts. Case had slept with Jade. Jade had given Case blowjobs. "I hear you play guitar," Case said, then asked what kind of guitar. I told him I'd been playing for a few years, mostly acoustic, but wasn't all that good.

"Hey, what are you guys talking about?" Jade said, crawling over excitedly, wedging herself between Case and I.

"We were talking about titties," Case said.

"Better be talking about mine, you queers."

"Show me your titties, woman."

Ty was laughing his ass off. He'd told me Case could get a little obnoxious if Jade was paying attention to other guys. Tries to pass it of as humour, you know? But, nah, you can tell he's pissed. Anyway, she likes to pay attention to all the new people around her.

NIGHT DIVIDES THE DAY

Jade asked if I had brought my guitar and Case said, "Did you see him bring a fucking guitar?" I didn't catch what Jade said to Case, but he moved over to J.P. and Jade began distracting herself with me. Again she put her mouth to my ear, paused, and said, "Hey, we'll go do some acid when we get there. We'll get blankets and... lie under the stars and..." she started to laugh, forgetting what she was going to say, called everyone *you fuckers*, said *it's going to be awesome*.

At the bottom of a hill, the pick up stopped and turned right. We disappeared into the forest.

"I don't know how you can sleep like that, man," Ty said. "My ass is killing me. God, I'm starving, too"

It was odd to leave the narrow back road, return to pavement, farmhouses, the river. It was odd to think we'd have to return to school tomorrow. I wondered if school would be cancelled, a day to mourn, but I knew it wouldn't.

I told Ty I wasn't sleeping, was thinking. The orchids. He started to tell me not to do too much of that, when we both heard Case mutter something. He was looking at Ty, kind of peering under his ball cap. "You're fucking hungry?" he said. "You're fucking hungry?"

Ty slid lower, said nothing.

Had Case and Jade spoken at all last night, after we got out of the pickup? When we arrived at the cabin, he went inside with J.P. and Serge and, far as I could tell, they drank beer, smoked pot, and played cards. Jade had again asked if anyone wanted to go make a campsite and drop acid and get fucked up but all she got back was *acid's for hippies* from Serge. "Fucking right," Jade responded. "So what are you fuckers going to do?" she then asked Ty and Corwin, who were talking about Corwin's truck, a gleaming black monster. Her tone had changed. I heard her say something under her breath about losers and then she turned to me.

"Don't tell me you want to stay here and jerk off about the truck?"

"God no," I said.

She grabbed her backpack and a fleece blanket from the pickup, then sent me to the cabin for more beer. Suddenly, I wasn't sure what the hell was going on. All the anticipation had crept away.

How many times had they done this before?

In the cabin they were sitting at the table, talking lowly. I asked where the cooler was and Serge pointed. "Derek," J.P. said. "How's it going?"

"Good," I said.

"Go do acid with Jade, keep her out of our hair."

I laughed, said she was hyper, yeah.

"Oh, that's nothing."

I left, feeling like a thief, the beer cradled to my chest. Case hadn't said a word, hadn't even looked up. Outside, we put the beer in the backpack, atop the blanket, and Jade gave me another high five. "Good man," she said. She slung the backpack over her shoulder.

It was hard to keep up with her, hard to see her if she was more than a few feet ahead. The path was thickly overgrown and Jade would stop, hold a branch, tell me to duck, and then keep on moving. I asked her where exactly we were going and she said to the creek, I think it's this way. You're not sure? I said. And she said nope, but who cares? Let's get the fuck out of here. I wanted to ask her if I had done something to upset her and she stopped, said wait. She took my hand.

"Follow me."

She was excited again.

She led me to a stand of trees, solitary and towering pines. She said she could feel them, wasn't it beautiful how they watched over you? I love this place more than anything. They're like... grandmothers, she said. Holding you, rocking you. They must be old, I said, and she asked if I could feel it too? It's peaceful, I said.

"Open your mouth."

"Why?"

"Stick your tongue out a little."

She wet her finger, dabbed it into her palm, and placed the tip of her finger on the tip of my tongue. "That's one hit," she said. "Hold it there and don't swallow, OK? Just keep it under your tongue—that way you can drink, too."

She gave me a beer from her backpack and we sat against one of the pines. We could hear the creek. For the longest time, we said nothing, and when I did start to speak, she hushed me. She said she was practicing her deep breathing. She said I should practice it too. So I breathed. I'm here with Jade, I was thinking. I'm sitting in the woods alone with Jade. Derek McDonald and Janice Bishop are side by side, alone, in the woods.

"We should never move from here, Jade."

"Hush."

Then we heard the cabin's screen door slam shut, so we moved deeper into the woods, the beer clinking in the backpack.

She crawled nude through the field, pretending she was a cat. Let's be cats, Derek. She cut her knee on a jagged bottle and was fascinated by the blood. She smeared the blood on my face. I couldn't stop telling her how beautiful she was. You're like the grass, and the stars, Jade. No, you're like the moon.

We wrestled in the field. Her dark hair was like a nest. Tiny, she was curled in it, crying.

I was standing in the field for hours, swaying with the wind. The sun is a cathedral, I thought. You can hear it. I have to tell Jade the sun is a cathedral.

There was whispering from the fields and I followed it, but I could not find Jade. Jade, I called. I wandered and found someone, near the creek, hanging in the dawn pines, but it wasn't Jade.

I found someone, but I never found Jade.

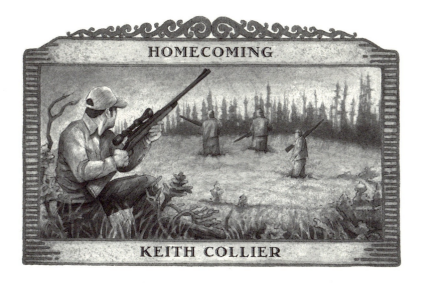

HOMECOMING

KEITH COLLIER

1

Jeremy was halfway through his first tour when a bomb outside the city's main market almost killed him. He didn't remember much, the vehicle pulling to the side of the road, then nothing.

He woke up in hospital four days later. He asked about his family, and was told they had been informed of his incident but that he was expected to recover. The doctors gave him a straight account of his injuries, how long it would take to heal, and what he would and wouldn't be able to do again.

He asked if he had any mail or phone calls. Mail would take a few days to catch up with him at the hospital, he was told, and several members of his family had called. He could call them back in a day or two, when he was feeling stronger.

The hospital in Germany was clean and busy, and strained with uncertainty and the pressure to heal, to become whole again. After his third surgery, Jeremy still had not heard from Jenn. The army had flown his mother over to see him a few days after the incident, and when he asked about Jenn, she just said that everybody home was doing fine.

Jenn was three weeks buried before his mother told him why he hadn't heard from her yet.

"I shouldn't have gone," he said, when his mother told him.

"You had to," his mother said. "Don't be ridiculous."

The hospital in Canada was more relaxed, the men and women coming to terms with their injuries, confident that they would heal, or that they wouldn't. Jeremy was released after two months, cautioned against strenuous activity, told to keep his physiotherapist appointments and to consider how lucky he was to still be in one piece.

Left arm in a sling, Jeremy flew home to Newfoundland, reflecting on the irony that while his body was being torn open by combat, it was Jenn who was dying, lying safe on her bathroom floor.

His father met him at the airport in St. John's, and drove him home.

***

The weather was warming around the bay, the first days of summer when it was almost warm enough to swim. Jeremy's old bedroom still had the same posters on the wall, the same model airplanes on the desk. His parents hadn't touched his room.

Jeremy was surprised by the number of old friends that were still around, some of them parents, some married, some not. Every day, somebody new dropped by to see him, chatting about what was happening in the community and their plans for the summer. He was uneasy about not being able to work, but determined to enjoy his time off. He had to heal.

One of those who visited was Jenn's brother, Darren, a quiet young man who asked him to go for a drink. It was strange, Jeremy thought, for the two had never really liked each other.

Darren was friendly, and bought Jeremy a beer when he arrived. The conversation naturally turned to Jenn, to a surprisingly comfortable reminiscence about summer camping trips, and about drinking around winter fires in the woods on nights so cold that the beer turned to slush before it could be finished.

The way people avoided talking about his injuries and about Jenn made them both more painful. Jeremy had begun to feel that he wanted somebody to say her name, just to prove she had existed, and he was glad that Darren had the will to talk about her, to keep her alive for him.

***

Jeremy had to drive to St. John's three times a week for physiotherapy, and to refill his prescriptions. The small local pharmacy didn't stock the painkillers he had been prescribed. The two hour drive was tiring, especially driving with one arm, but it gave structure to his week, gave him something to do either today or tomorrow, a routine to follow.

***

Jeremy was relieved when Jenn's mother invited him over for dinner. He had been planning to see her, but he hadn't been able to face crossing that threshold yet. The invitation made the decision for him, and he knew she would appreciate the visit. Jenn's mother had always liked him.

She made lasagna, knowing how much Jeremy liked it but making too much as usual since her husband was gone back to Alberta. His work rotation brought him home for four weeks out of every ten, and he always came home the first day of his break, and stayed until the last possible moment. Her house was clean and too quiet, even with the television on in the background.

Over dinner, they were both painfully aware that this was the first time Jeremy was in her house without Jenn's comforting intermediary presence, someone through whom they could relate to each other.

Without her between them, their relationship was unclear and undefined. The conversation was strained with Jeremy's unspoken questions and her mother's unspoken answers. She asked him how his mother was doing, and what his tour had been like. What was it like being in a foreign country?

The only questions he could think of, and the only questions he felt he could bring himself to ask, were about Jenn. Had she finished her application to university yet? Had she heard back from jobs she had applied for? These were questions that were no longer relevant, that had no meaningful answers anymore, and Jeremy kept silent.

He helped with the dishes after dinner, and her mother made tea. She made it in a teapot, and Jeremy felt like it was part of a routine, a preparation for something. She moved around the kitchen as if performing a drill, getting the tea and the cups and the sugar in a practiced way that had a definite end.

She asked him if he would like to look around Jenn's room, and he understood what that end was. She had been preparing herself to ask him this, perhaps feeling that he was owed this opportunity. He could take anything he liked, she said, pictures or letters or anything that meant something to him. He knew that she hadn't touched a thing in that room, that he would be the first person to disturb the remains of Jenn's life since she had died, and he knew that this was a big step for her mother, perhaps the first admission that she was truly gone.

He went into her room and sat down, looking around at the mess on the dresser, the pile of laundry on the floor, and the books by her bed, and he wanted to take everything with him, every item of furniture and every article of clothing and put them back together somewhere where he could guard it and keep it exactly the way it was for the rest of his life. He had forgotten the smell of her room, that particular blend of fresh laundry, perfume and lotions, the comforting scent of her. Her bed was still unmade, possibly with the same sheets he had slept in the night before he left for St. John's to board the plane.

***

The first time he had spent the night in Jenn's room, they were both seventeen. Her mother was away in St. John's at a conference, her mother's boyfriend, and soon-to-be husband, in Alberta. They rented movies from the convenience store and watched them in her room, feeling too strange sitting in the empty living room, the flickering blue light from the television the only light in the room until they fell asleep with the first light of dawn at the curtains. They made a breakfast of pancakes when they woke up, and Jeremy was gone by the time Jenn's mother returned home around noon.

They had cleaned up well, washing the dishes, taking out the garbage and returning the movies, so that no trace of his visit remained in the house. But the house had been too clean when she returned, too orderly, and her mother had known.

***

Jeremy took her backpack from where Jenn had thrown it behind the door. First he placed his own clothes in it, random clothes left scattered around the room after three years of weekend nights in her bed. A sweater, a couple of T-shirts, some socks.

Then there was a shoebox full of letters, the pictures she had stuck in her mirror, an old T-shirt that she liked to sleep in, her favourite books and the condoms from the bedside table. They all went into her backpack. He took her diary from under the bed and placed it on top, zipping the backpack closed. He said goodnight to her mother and went home, Jenn's backpack slung over his right shoulder because his left was still healing and still too weak to bear the weight.

HOMECOMING

***

His shoulder was throbbing the next morning, and he had the last of his painkillers for breakfast. He would get the prescription refilled in St. John's. It would be the first time he finished the bottle of pills in a single week in the month that he had been taking them.

He drove to St. John's for his physiotherapist appointment, his left arm resting on the door and steering almost entirely with his right. By the time he arrived, his right arm was stiff and sore, cramped from being constantly raised and the minute movements of highway driving.

His appointment with the physiotherapist was the same as always. She asked him questions about how much pain he felt, how his exercises were going. She tested his range of motion, and was pleased to note a slight improvement over last week.

Jeremy left her office and went to the drugstore, refilling his prescription. Then he went to meet Joanne for lunch. She arrived just in time to see him wash down the first of that batch of pills.

Jeremy hadn't seen Joanne in months. She had called a few days earlier, and wanted to meet for coffee or for lunch. She was a nurse at a hospital in St. John's, and with Jeremy's physiotherapy schedule, arranging to meet was easy.

She asked about his injuries, about the pain. Jeremy answered that he was healing, that the pain was manageable.

Seeing her made his chest tighten, the way it felt when he woke after dreaming about the bright dusty roadside in Afghanistan again. She looked so much like her sister that when she walked into the restaurant, Jeremy was certain it was Jenn come to meet him on a break from her classes.

She hugged him when she approached, jokingly complimenting his tan, breaking the tension Jeremy was feeling. They sat at a table in the back, talking quietly, and when she reached to pick up the sugar with her right hand, the white gold engagement ring would catch the dim light, tightening Jeremy's chest again.

She saw him notice it. "I've been wearing it," she said. "Did you want it back?" She started to take it off.

Jeremy stopped her. "No, you keep it," he said. "What would I do with it?"

She asked him what he planned to do now that he was home, and he told her he had no idea. He had to take more time off before he was strong enough to work.

He wanted to ask if she knew anything, if she could tell him anything about Jenn, about why she had taken her own life, why, when he was being loaded into that helicopter on a stretcher, she had gone into the kitchen for the paring knife.

"I feel like she knew what had happened to me somehow, that it's my fault," he said. "Like she had gone for the knife out of despair."

"It wasn't your fault," Joanne said to him. "Something was very wrong. She wouldn't tell me what. I tried to ask, but she wouldn't talk about it."

"I wish I could know."

"Me too," she said. "Mom told me you took her diary?"

"I haven't read it yet."

"Read it," Joanne said. "Maybe it will help."

"Maybe it will make it worse."

"Maybe. But I don't think there are any secrets she wanted to keep from you."

Joanne kept brushing hair from her forehead as she spoke, a mannerism she had shared with her sister. She saw him wince as he reached for the sugar. Sometimes it was the smallest movements that caused the greatest pain.

***

The weekend after he met with Joanne, Jenn's mother was gone to St. John's for a conference, and her house was empty.

HOMECOMING

Jeremy took the shoebox of letters and the diary back to Jenn's house, letting himself in through the never-locked front door. He went into Jenn's room, closing the door behind him and sitting down on the bed.

Most of the letters he didn't read. Many were from him anyway, sent to her while he was in basic training or posted to Gagetown. There were letters from her sister, from friends who had moved away, letters from old boyfriends. These last he did not read. They were before his time, and he was not jealous.

The diary was mostly what he had expected, records of her fights with her siblings and her mother, long entries describing their fights in detail, and painful descriptions of the weekends they had spent in bed together. She hadn't written much after she left for St. John's to go to school, perhaps not having the time, or seeing the diary as a school girl's habit.

The last entry was dated three days before the bomb changed Jeremy's life forever. It was addressed to him, a draft of a letter that she had never sent.

Joanne's bond with Jenn had been strong, and her sister's intuition had not been wrong. When Jeremy saw the words written down in front of him, written down for him to read, he saw the physical act as if it was happening right in front of him, on the very bed on which he sat.

It had happened so fast, she wrote. He had knocked on her door, the two of them alone in the house, wanting to ask her about something but clearly distracted, not able to focus on what he was saying or what she was saying in reply. She had tried to cry out, but was muffled by the pillow, muffled by the empty house and her own confusion and surprise.

Jenn and Jeremy hadn't had sex before he had been deployed. She hadn't wanted to, and Jeremy didn't want to push it, didn't want to start a fight the day before he left. They hadn't had sex in almost six weeks, since the night before he left for his last round of training before his deployment to Afghanistan, and she had had her period a week later.

While Jeremy was being tended to by frantic and efficient medics on a dusty roadside in Kabul, while his nervous comrades set up a perimeter around the stricken vehicle, firing warning shots at anything that moved, Jenn was peeing on a stick in her bathroom. The medics were under pressure to get him ready to move quickly so they could withdraw, and Jenn was sitting on the edge of her bathtub, waiting for the answer.

***

The new cemetery was flatter than the old one, located on a field behind the church, rather than on a hillside overlooking the harbour. The grass was well kept and the headstones were in orderly rows. The weeks of rain and wind had settled the mound of dirt on her grave so that it was almost flat, with shoots of new green grass showing through. It was September, and frost would soon kill the last of her flowers.

"What do I do?" he asked her.

In the damp, cool fall air he could feel the bones of his arm knitting back together, and it hurt. He had left his pills at home, and he turned to leave.

2

"Do you hunt?" Jenn's uncle Rob asked him, late one Saturday night at the pub. He, Jeremy and Darren were out for a night of drinking and pool. Rob had lived with Jenn and her mother for the last couple of years.

"I haven't in a while," Jeremy answered. "But I used to."

"I've got my moose license this year," her uncle said. "And Darren got one for caribou. We'll be going as soon as the season starts and Bill gets back from Alberta. Want to come?"

Jeremy thought about hiking through the woods and over the marshes again, rubber boots sucking in the bog and a backpack full of bologna sandwiches and Vienna sausages, the weight of a rifle in his arms. "I'd love to get out in the woods again."

HOMECOMING

Darren laughed. "I'll bet you're a great shot," he said.

Jeremy went outside for a cigarette, feeling the pain in his shoulder. He had taken as many painkillers as he dared while drinking, and it seemed that drinking made it worse.

Joanne was home for the weekend, and she followed him outside. "Can I have one of those?" she asked. Jeremy handed one over.

"I didn't know you smoked," he said.

"I don't," she answered, lighting the cigarette from the end of his. "Have you read Jenn's diary yet?"

"No," he lied. "I still can't bring myself to."

"I understand," Joanne said, "I guess there's no rush," even though she didn't understand, thought Jeremy. She didn't understand at all.

***

The first weekend in October, Jeremy got ready to go hunting. He had packed his army backpack with food and water, a small first aid kit, dry socks, and the handful of other things he would need, packing with a methodical discipline that came from training. He had borrowed a hunting jacket from Jenn's uncle, and he had his father's old Italian .308 rifle, his pockets full of cartridges. Leaving the house, he automatically checked the safety, even though the gun wasn't loaded yet.

He met the hunting party at Jenn's, her brother Darren, her stepfather Bill and her uncle Rob. They were loaded into two pickup trucks, each carrying an ATV and the supplies of food and beer. They would travel by ATV to a hunting lodge, and then spend as many days as it took hunting on foot through the inland bogs and barrens. Nobody expected them back for at least three or four days.

The pickup trucks rattled over the old logging road. Jeremy was driving with Darren, the two older men in the other truck ahead. Darren was smoking a cigarette while he drove, avoiding the deep puddles and the larger rocks.

"What are you hunting with?" he asked.
"My father's .308," Jeremy said.
"That old sniper rifle?"
"That's right."
"Great gun. You'll never miss with that."
"I hope not," Jeremy said.

They reached the end of the road. The men unloaded the ATVs, strapping coolers and boxes to the racks. Jeremy climbed on behind Darren, and they set off for the hunting lodge.

They reached it about an hour later, twelve miles from the logging road and twenty-five from town. They unpacked the food and the beer, cooking supper and drinking until midnight.

They were up at dawn, frying bacon and smoking cigarettes in the cool fall morning. Jeremy's shoulder was throbbing, but the weight of the pack when he put it on wasn't bad. They set out for the trails, splitting into two groups, Jeremy going with Darren again, making friendly bets as to who would bag their animal first.

It was barely ten o'clock in the morning when the first crack of a rifle shot split the air, followed closely by another. It wasn't far off, probably less than a mile, and Jeremy and Darren set out at a quick trot in the direction of the shot.

They reached the dead animal before Bill and Rob, the moose having bolted towards them before collapsing. Rob was congratulating himself on the shot, Bill arguing that it was his bullet that had brought the big male down. They had both fired, and Jeremy pointed out two sets of wounds in the animal's hide. Both men had made their shots, one hitting the moose through the chest and the other further back, a gut shot that may have ruined some of the meat.

Rob took out his skinning knife and bled the animal. Bill dug out the Coleman stove and the kettle, and Darren made tea. When they had eaten their lunch, Bill and Rob gutted the moose while Darren went back to the lodge to get the ATV. Jeremy wielded the small camp axe, the sharp blade cutting

HOMECOMING

easily through ribs and muscle as he quartered the animal and finished dressing it to transport back to the lodge.

For dinner that night, they had a moose roast, a big cut of meat with potatoes and gravy. Drinking beer after dinner, Jeremy took one of the other roasts they had cut from the moose before hanging it in the meat shed, and cut it into strips, using a razor sharp boning knife that he found in the cutlery drawer. He fried it with onions and garlic, a bedtime snack.

They were up at dawn again the next day, having breakfast and setting out early. "It's our turn today," Darren said, as the two groups separated. "We'll be feasting on fresh caribou tonight."

"We'll see," said Rob, he and Bill heading off into the woods.

It didn't take long for Darren to spot some caribou tracks. "See," he said. "We'll get ours before lunch, you watch."

The tracks were fresh, made sometime in the very early morning. They quickened their pace, following the trail down to the brook, up the bank on the other side, and across the bog to a grove of trees.

Jeremy saw it first. A huge animal, bigger than the one they had shot yesterday, and definitely not a caribou. "Jesus," said Darren. "He's huge. Come on!"

"We've already got the moose," said Jeremy. "Caribou trail goes that way."

"I don't care," said Darren. "I'm not letting that one get away. Won't be the first time we've brought out a six-quartered moose. We can track down the caribou later. Come on!"

They moved through the woods, keeping downwind of the moose, closing the distance. They were about 100 yards away when Darren stopped, raised his rifle and braced himself against a tree.

Darren fired, and Jeremy saw the tree leaves shudder above the animal's back, the moose starting and moving away. Jeremy brought his father's rifle to his shoulder, flicking the safety off and firing in a smooth motion before Darren had even re-cocked his own rifle.

The moose stumbled, kneeling onto its front legs before struggling back to its feet and disappearing into the trees.

Darren and Jeremy ran towards the moose, breaking through the trees where the animal had gone, seeing blood on the leaves. They could see the moose close by, head hanging low, settling to his knees. Jeremy had chambered another round in the rifle, ready to finish the animal off.

Bill and Rob came through the trees right next to the dying moose, drawn by the shots. The moose was obviously still alive, though it had collapsed onto its side.

Jeremy yelled at the two men to get out of the way so he could deliver the final shot. They were too close, and the wounded moose kicked out, catching Bill on the leg just below the knee and cracking the bone with a crunch. Bill collapsed next to the moose, and Jeremy shot the animal behind the ear.

The bones of Bill's leg were protruding through his skin and blood was soaking into his pants. Jeremy tore his pant leg open and examined the injury.

"Belt," he said, pointing to Darren. Darren gave him his belt and Jeremy fashioned a tourniquet, twisting it around Bill's leg, as he groaned with the pain.

"We've got to get him to the hospital," Jeremy said. "This is bad."

"I can be back with the ATV in an hour," said Darren.

"I'd better go too," said Rob. "If I get the other ATV, we can bring the moose out too."

"Go," said Jeremy.

"Keep your rifle handy," said Darren. "We've still got a caribou to get, and we know they're handy."

***

When she was sixteen, Jenn would spend as many weekends as possible sleeping over at a friend's house, or with her father and her sister in St. John's, and they would stay up late watching movies and eating popcorn and ice cream. They

HOMECOMING

would talk about school and sports, boys and makeup, the subject matter not changing much as she turned from sixteen to seventeen to eighteen, Jenn glad to be out of the house and away from Bill's uncomfortable presence. She thought it had gotten better as she grew up and when she moved away, but she soon realized that it was Jeremy's presence that had changed things. Jeremy knew that Bill made Jenn uncomfortable, and that he was afraid of Jeremy.

After she turned eighteen, she moved to St. John's, staying with her father and her sister while she went to class, and when she was home for long weekends and holidays, Jeremy would stay over and they would sleep late. Bill was always an early riser and would be gone by the time they got up to get breakfast, gone to the cabin or in the country cutting wood.

When Jenn and Jeremy had first started dating at sixteen, Bill would pick up the phone extension while they talked, not saying anything but refusing to acknowledge his presence when she screamed at him to get off the phone. Sometimes he would make lewd comments, or threats. Once he asked her to forgive him, and even at sixteen, Jeremy knew there was something seriously wrong with what had been said.

He and Jeremy had gotten into their only fight just before high school graduation, and he had backed down quickly. Bill came back with a souvenir bullet, his name inscribed on it, and said that he didn't want to live like this, with people hating him and not forgiving him, and that the bullet had his name on it for a reason.

Jeremy had taken the bullet with Bill's name on it before he left on the hunting trip.

***

Jeremy dug an apple out of his backpack, cutting slices off it with his pocketknife. He offered some to Bill, who was lying propped against a tree, eyes closed and sweating.

Bill couldn't eat. "Jesus, it hurts," he said.

"Here," said Jeremy, getting out his pills and some water. "Take a couple of those and you'll be feeling fine in no time."

Bill took the pills, swallowing them with water and leaning back against the tree.

"I'm going to loosen your tourniquet a bit, okay?" said Jeremy. "Check on the bleeding."

Bill just grunted. The bleeding had slowed considerably, and Jeremy left the tourniquet loose.

"I guess you learned all this first aid stuff in the army, huh?" Bill asked, when Jeremy had finished.

"Everybody knows first aid in the army," he said. "And we had extra training before we deployed."

"Did you ever kill anyone over there?" Bill asked, the pills starting to work.

"No," said Jeremy.

"Too bad," said Bill. "That would have been quite the experience, huh?"

"I'll bet it would have," he said.

They were silent for a while.

"She was pregnant you know."

The pills weren't strong enough to hide Bill's reaction. "What?" he said.

"Jenn," said Jeremy. "She was pregnant. That's why she did it. She couldn't stand it."

"But you weren't going to be gone that long..." Bill began.

"It wasn't mine." Jeremy reached into his pocket. "Remember this?" he said, holding up the bullet with the name inscribed on it. "You were right. It had your name on it for a reason."

He opened the bolt of his father's rifle, and slid the round into the chamber. He could hear the first drones of the ATVs, of Darren and Rob's return. He closed the bolt, taking off the safety.

His finger was on the trigger. Jeremy could see the ATVs now, approaching from the other side of the bog.

"You killed us both," he said.

HOMECOMING

The shot sounded across the bog, and Darren stopped the ATV. "What the hell was that?" he said to Rob. "You think Jeremy got the caribou, too?"

SKY

JOANNE SOPER-COOK

Floyd Carcassian jumped from the seventh floor of the hospital at six o'clock this morning. I was still asleep when he did it: dozing in the chilly air of late November, while the moon seated itself behind the hills and dawn came crawling slowly from out of the steel grey ocean.

I remember Floyd on the day I met him: standing outside of O'Brien's, contemplating a display of accordians in the window. It was already November, but the sun was shining, and most of us had left our desks this lunch hour, to stroll up Water Sreet and Duckworth, breathe a little of the salty air. The stiff nor'easter didn't manage to blow away the stench, exhaled from the harbour's foul throat, and whenever I think of Floyd, I always remember him surrounded by a vestige of that smell—lingering about him like a miasma, or a halo.

Floyd worked in my building, just two floors down, in Births, Marriages and Deaths—"Cradle to Grave," we called it, as if that were somehow funny. Floyd always managed to be on the elevator at the same time I was—examining his face, the folds of his neck, in the polished brass fitments. He'd nod and suck his teeth at me, the only kind of greeting that I ever remember us exchanging. When I passed by the buzzing hive of desks and cubicles that formed his office, I often glimpsed the pale back of his neck, as he sat with his head bent, going over stacks of forms. He had that air of thoroughness about him, as if he alone possessed the necessary mental fortitude required for the job.

I remember that he wore spectacles: fashionable spectacles, mere loops of glass and wire, invisibly balanced on the very center of his fleshy nose; twin moons suspended by an ephemera of glass.

"Sure is a nice day, what?" I'd positioned myself directly next to his right elbow, feigned interest in the accordians. The speakers overhead blared a noxious mixture of Celtic and Country Western, sung by a man with a bazooka for a nose, whose photographic representation graced the swinging doors. Patrons moving in or out of the building were thus forced to place their sweating palms directly in his unearthly visage and push, until he fell away, and the confines of his glassed-in world admitted them. "Wind's a bit cold, though." I adjusted the collar of my coat to punctuate this most laudatory truth; my words achieved a conspiratorial taint, simply because I found myself leaning close to Floyd in order to wring some sort of response from him.

"Cold." He coughed delicately into his hand, shoved the offending digits into the pocket of his trousers, and pointedly ignored me. He seemed enthralled with the display of accordians, and leaned far forward until his nose nearly pressed against the glass.

"Thinking of taking up that, are you?" I jerked my head towards the instruments. "Going to play at weddings and stuff like that?"

"I do not play." It was uttered with the same ponderous intensity; he seemed incapable of any other mood. I imagined him late at night, sorting through the boxes of files down in the basement, a single light bulb flaring into life above him. He would do everything with furrowed brow, his lower lip clenched between his rodent teeth, intense. "I had planned to become a commercial pilot." He didn't bother to look at me.

"Bad eyes, huh?" I understood: I was as blind as the proverbial bat myself, but managed to camouflage my disability with contact lenses. I have often argued it is because I thus see better, but in my most secret soul, I know that I am simply vain, as few men are. Rob tells me it is one of my endearing traits, but I often suppose he makes up such lies to placate me, and because we live together.

"Have you ever really looked at the sky?" He turned and gazed fully at me, something that seemed to cause him pain, because he winced a little. His chin burrowed further into the collar of his shirt, shrinking from me. Perhaps he regretted his disclosure; I never heard him speak more than a handful of words in a sentence. Even his workday discourse was uttered in short, sharp, monosyllabic bursts. "When you gaze at the sky, it gazes back. Such blue. Have you ever thought of that?"

I blinked, a plethora of blinks to clear my mind. He seemed to be fading backwards in my gaze, disappearing into the jingling midday air. The music had stopped. There was nothing now but the afternoon hum of downtown traffic, taxicabs and buses. "The sky."

"I have to go now." He nodded at me curtly, wheeled upon his heels like an army officer might do, and marched off in the opposite direction. He was heading away from our building, away from his work, and as he went, I noticed how his slender back was bent and bowed a little, as if under the weight of an invisible burden.

When I got back to my desk, there was a line of people waiting, and so I didn't get a chance to think about Floyd at all. A man in a battered yellow baseball cap was first in line, clutching a greasy slip of paper between his meaty fingers. I thought about Floyd's delicate pink digits, shoved into the pocket of his trousers. "I'm puttin' a back deck on me house." He shoved the paper at me, then stood abruptly back from the desk, as if I and my surroundings contained some kind of breathable taint, with which he would become infected. A lot of them acted this way; it had nothing to do with me and my personal life, with Rob and I—although, at one time I thought it had. I thought that people could see through my hastily-contrived facade, but Rob assured me that this was not so. "How could they?" he'd asked me, with an expression of disgust and amusement. "It's not like you're wearing a dress, for god's sake!" It was true: I was as well turned out as all the others; there was nothing strange or unusual about my dress, my manner. I did not—as Rob had asserted—show up at work in women's garb, nor was I inclined in that direction, although tradition and social agreement dictates that such is the expected mode of dress. I fit in well here, and I liked my job—even meeting Floyd in the elevator, which at least lent a moment or two of interest to my day.

It was four o'clock before I even thought about Floyd again; Ellen Bronson from Purchasing stopped by my desk with her purse. "You going down for a smoke, or what?" I indicated that I would, felt hurridly in my coat pocket for cigarettes and lighter.

"Jack Tizzard is some pissed off this afternoon. Whooo, by the Jesus!" Ellen didn't wait till we got outside to light her smoke, but fizzed a match into existence in the elevator. "I suppose you never heard, did ya?" Her eyes were pale green, a pleasant colour, and fixed me in their gaze. I liked Ellen—she was one of the few in which I had confided. When I'd told her the truth, she'd patted my arm and grinned at me, "Nothing wrong with it, my duckie. But you might want to keep your head down around here. You know what the boss is like."

"Heard what?" I knew immediately that it had something to do with Floyd.

"Floyd Carcassian." Ellen jerked her shoulders in that gesture she had: it meant everything from *piss off and leave me alone* to *come here till I tells you something*. "Never came back to work after dinner. Jack says if he comes back, he's fired anyway. Or at the very least, he's getting a note in his file for it."

We moved out of the comparitive gloom into the sunshine of late afternoon. Soon it would be getting dark early, as the sun spun away from us, disappearing into space for a span of time. I hated it, that dark time, when everything stilled and the earth died a little. Rob always told me not to be so foolish, that it was a time of resting and regeneration. His religion believed in things like that. I had had no religion for as long as I cared to remember. I didn't believe in resting, or regeneration. Things didn't rest, they died.

"Where did he go?" I asked.

Ellen was immersed in watching a wino fish half-empty bottles out of a garbage can, and didn't answer for a moment. The late sun struck sparks into her green eyes, like pale emeralds: jewels laid out for display that nobody cared about and nobody wanted. "Nobody knows. Mike Green said he's pobably gone up on Signal Hill to see if he can fly!" Her face disintegrated into raucous laughter; with a murmured apology, I shoved myself away from the warm brick wall.

I was just in time to catch the elevator: Floyd's boss, Jack Tizzard, was inside, glaring spitefully at the contents of his briefcase. "How are ya?" he asked. He was short and rotund, with the face of a suckling pig. His beefy forearms strained at the rolled-up sleeves of his shirt.

I wanted to ask him about Floyd, but I didn't dare. "Not bad, boy. Nice afternoon out there."

I sniffed my clothing furtively: did I smell like cigarette smoke, like late-afternoon sun, and the stench of rot from the harbour?

"Some Jesus cold, though." He laughed, a surprisingly hearty sound. "Soon be snow up to your arse, I daresay."

"Yes, boy." I couldn't think of anything else to say; I was immured in disastrous thoughts.

When the lighted buttons showed my floor, I moved to exit, then stopped. "How's Floyd these days?"

SKY

The elevator door opened; I shoved the toe of my shoe between the sensors to keep it open. I was good at stalling tactics such as these. Rob said I could go on and on for weeks without so much as mentioning the truth. He only accepted my lies, my facile explanations, because he loved me, he said. Perhaps we had grown comfortable with each other.

"Floyd who?" Jack pressed his face close to mine, examined me.

The door slid slowly closed, bumped gently against my foot. "Uh, never mind." I slipped my hand between the closing doors. When I stopped at the corner to glance back, the car had already gone up, carrying Jack Tizzard and all his secrets, safe in a building like this, a hive.

I had some difficulty with the last few steps of the trail; I hadn't climbed up here for years, and certainly not by myself. Sometimes in the summer, when it was hot and we were dying for a breath of fresh air, Rob and I would take the Jeep up to the top, and sit on the low stone wall, and look out at the Atlantic ocean. "That's Ireland, over there," Rob would say, just so I could pretend to look for it on the bald face of the horizon. "That's where my grandfather came from, and yours." We were all Irish here, or pretended to be: it went with the accent, with the attitude, with the cloistered Catholic mentality of a city that felt itself to be a small town.

I couldn't stay up here very long: the sun would soon be setting and the wind was bloody cold, blowing through my overcoat like cast-off knives. Already the horizon was ablaze with light, a violent red sun being devoured by the sea and thousands of clouds. I felt like I had to look at the sky, like there was something in it for me to see, something that I hadn't seen before. It was the same impulse that made me step close to the edge of the cliff and gaze down into the abyss, six hundred feet to the steel-grey sea. "Why do you do that?" Rob asked me, once. "Why do you step to the edge and stare at it like that? Sure, there's nothing to see." Rob worked in a bank: he had an office of his own, and a fake mahogany desk, and the girls in the office all got together on his birthday and gave him a big bouquet of flowers and a bottle of Captain Morgan. He liked things to be orderly, to make sense; I pretended that I liked these things, as well. I always knew how it would be with Rob: that I would be safe, and secure, that I could always count on him to be tomorrow exactly as he was today. There would be no unsettling elements. Life would proceed forward, a series of small, carefully-prescribed steps. He kept our basement apartment spotless, because I have no head for cleaning, or else I forget: I would dust the bureau once or twice a month with a balled-up sweat sock, swirl some Javex around in the toilet bowl. Rob liked the curtains closed all the time, even at night. He said it was cosy, that it made the apartment seem more homey. I'd rather have them open, and the windows too, even in the winter. He got furious with me once when he came home late on a Friday night and our bed was covered in half an inch of snow. If I slept with the windows open, then the sky could come in, and it didn't seem so much like I was living underground, hiding like a mole, listening for the footfall of vibration in the ground above me. It's safe to come out now!

Floyd wasn't up here. I didn't know what Ellen had been on about. He wasn't here, or at least his car wasn't here. Where did she get that idea, I wondered. Maybe somebody said something about Floyd coming up here. I should have asked Jack Tizzard, but I didn't have the nerve.

The wind was picking up; I should go down, I thought. In a minute I was going to be swept off the cliffs, dashed against the hard walls of the ocean below. The freshening breeze descended into chill, and lifted the tails of my overcoat. Below, on the trail, there was a sheer drop, and no handrail, but merely a chain let into the cliff. If I held on and arched my other side out over the sea, the wind might lift me and I might fly like Icarus. Perhaps I could soar into the sky, well above the ground. I was like Napoleon on St. Helena, chained to the rock.

I leaned into the wind, cupped my hands around my mouth. "Fl—" My inhaled breath escaped me, useless. What would I say to him? What could I possibly say? And it was crazy anyway: there was no evidence that he was here. The only one up here was me, braving the November gale and gazing down into the inscrutable abyss. The wind was a swirling mass, astonishing: there was nowhere to hide up here, no need to hide underground like animals, afraid of daylight's cold stare. It's safe to come out now.

When I got home, Rob was already there, stirring something in a pot on the stove. I took off my overcoat and stowed it in the closet, hung my scarf on the same hanger, shucked my boots. The heat was delicious. "Where were you?" he asked. I squashed him to me and kissed him, pressed my cold nose against his cheek.

"Some bloody cold outside! Whew!" I rubbed my hands together in a show of briskness, of good cheer. The smell of the cooking pot permeated the room; this was what home smelled like. "I missed the goddamn bus," I explained.

"You can take the Jeep, you know." He grinned at me. "It's your car, too."

We ate in front of the TV set, while the news was on. It seemed like every night somebody robbed some place, stole things that didn't belong to them, and raced away into the dark with it. The announcer had vivid blue eyes, like the sky in the morning, unsettling. I wondered if perhaps the television cameras made it appear that way; sometimes things seem to exist, when in fact they don't.

When Rob and I went to bed, I left the window open.

I didn't hear about it until I was back at work the next day. Rob got up early to go for a run, and by the time I'd stumbled out of bed and into the shower, it was too late to put the radio on.

During the night, a fresh new snow had fallen, and coated everything with white. The sky was blinding blue, glaring off the white, an arctic chill. Nobody spoke on the bus: the heaters bayed and whined as we motored past the dark confines of LeMarchant, tipped down the stiff incline of Casey Street, and down into the grey pit near the harbour.

I had a pile of stuff to get through, and already there was a line of people at the desk, all clutching slips of greasy paper, creased and torn. *I wants a shed in me backyard,* and *Fauder said I got to get a permit to make a doghouse,* and *How far towards the sidewalk can the front porch go before I got to take it down?*

I didn't think of Floyd until I ran into Ellen near the elevator, clutching her pack of cigarettes and waiting for me. "Going down for a smoke?" she asked. It was cold today, and we'd both taken our coats with us; I wondered how I was going to smoke with gloves on.

She waited until we were outside. "I suppose you never heard," she said. She couldn't light her cigarette in the wind, and so I did it for her, lit it off the tip of mine, like passing the breath of life between us.

"What?"

"Floyd killed himself this morning. Jumped out the window of the hospital. Went up to visit his uncle on Third Medicine, had his gallbladder out." She sucked hard on her cigarette, watching me, and I noticed for the first time that her green eyes were cold and predatory, like the eyes of evil birds. "What do you think of that?"

I stuttered something, I don't know what it was, and fled. I didn't even stop to take my briefcase from my desk, I simply turned and walked into the hard November wind. The sky was grey, grey like the rocks below me, and I crouched with my back against the cliff and smoked a succession of endless cigarettes. The sea churned at my feet, a sheer drop to the bottom: perhaps the cold felt warm when you hit it from so high a distance. Perhaps the sky felt warm like that, and if you balanced delicately on the edge of a cliff, you might imagine that you could fly. Maybe spread your arms like wings and float for just a moment, like Icarus. When you gaze at the sky, it gazes back. That's what he said to me. The gaze of the abyss.

Somebody came from downstairs and cleaned his desk out, some guy in coveralls and dirty work boots, pushing a broom. "Floyd Carcassian's stuff?" It was contained in a small cardboard box, everything he'd brought with him, everything he owned. The janitor held it aloft like a holy relic, waved the box so that the contents rattled. "Anybody want this before I throws it out?" He'd brought it up to us, even though none of us had worked with Floyd. I only knew him on the elevator. "Anybody want it?"

Ellen darted forward slightly, but drew back at the last moment; I could see her visibly restraining herself. There was nothing in that box that she could understand.

"Nobody wants it?" He gathered it to him and shuffled down the corridor. Near where the elevator stops, I heard him whistling, The Black Velvet Band. I noticed Ellen watching me, standing with a group of secretaries near the coffee pot in the staff lounge. She was bent towards them and whispering. I wondered what she was saying, and then I didn't care.

I think about Floyd sometimes, when I'm up on the cliffs in the morning. Rob says I should exercise more and try to quit smoking, because he's not looking after me when I'm old and dying of lung cancer. I treat myself to a covert cigarette after my hike, crouching against the wind behind Cabot Tower, holding the match inside my coat to shield it from the wind. I think we might move out of the basement apartment, Rob and I. We just bought a new TV, and the living room is much too small for it. We might move out, and get a better place together, where I can leave the windows open and see the sky.

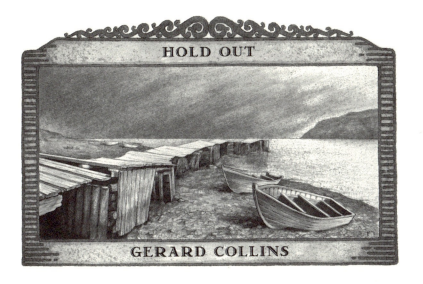

HOLD OUT

GERARD COLLINS

From the darkness of the shed, she observed the harbour. The rickety government wharf was littered with scowling men whose boats were tied up at the dock. Gazing out to the ocean, they appeared not to listen to each other, but talked only to remind themselves they were still alive. A brown beagle scampered among them, barking incessantly. Winnie wished the dog would shut up for once. It was getting on her nerves.

She could just imagine the conversations:
She's gone, b'ys, she's gone and
Who do she think she is? and
I wonder whatever happened to wassisname that used to be handy with the tools.

There was a time when she couldn't have stood such talk. Francis wouldn't have, that's for sure. He used to get so mad at the crowd who'd given up, who thought that the olden days were the only good days, and nothing worthwhile would ever come again. The young ones were nearly all gone, leaving mostly the old ones like herself to bury the dead and turn off the lights at the ends of days.

Even Francis was departed now, leaving her with an empty house and sitting here on a handmade bench in his musty shed with sawdust on the floor, cobwebs in the rafters, an unfinished boat in the back, and a litter of dead flies in the window sill. Still, it was the best view of the bay in the entire community.

A gentle knock on the door frame startled her. The silhouette of a woman standing in the entrance made her wonder what it would be like if an angel came to get her one of these days. Francis might not have believed in God, but Winnie managed to keep her faith all these years, despite some trying times.

The visitor stepped forward, her features far from angelic. On the contrary, it was a sullen face, scarred with the worry of thirty-odd years of having a husband and three sons who worked on the sea. Her skin was pock-marked, and her eyes had that faraway look that comes from perpetually scanning the horizon a dozen times a day for signs of a trawler with four of her men on board. It had been a few years since those days, but these were worrying times too, and some habits are performed perpetually, like a mask worn for so long that it becomes the true face.

"Angela." Winnie's tone was terse. She knew what Angela Downey was here for—same thing she always wanted. Why wouldn't that woman take no for an answer?

"Well, good morning to you too, Winnie. The committee sent me to talk to you."

Winnie sighed and picked at a loose sliver of wood on the sawhorse beside her. She considered it new, and yet Francis had made that sawhorse nearly ten years ago. "I did all my talking last night."

"Would you just listen to reason?" Coming in from the breeze, Angela dashed a hand through her bleach blonde hair. In Winnie's mind, the other woman was too old to be dying her hair—*not foolin' anyone*—but at least she could do her roots, if she was going to be at it. *A little neglect can bring down kingdoms*, she thought.

"I was just going in for a nap. So if you'll excuse me." Winnie swallowed hard and began the laborious process of getting to her feet. Steadying herself by holding onto the edge of the sawhorse, she leaned her elbow on its rough plane for leverage, and hauled her trembling frame to a nearly upright position until she was standing solidly. She shuffled towards the door while Angela was talking at her.

The visitor had to pivot in order to look the older woman in the face. "The time has come, Winnie. We can't hold out any longer."

Winnie stopped nearly in front of her. "Do you think I don't know that? Do you think I could forget even for one minute what they're asking us to do?" She laid a calming hand to her chest, remembering what the doctor had said about blood pressure.

"They're not asking us anything. We're the ones. There's no one left anymore. Hardly any young ones. No work. No store. No bank. Nothin' to do except clean the house, walk the streets, and watch television. There's no place to go. Not even a school or a church no more."

"We got schools," said Winnie. "We got a church too."

"But what good are they without a teacher or a priest?"

"Same good they always were, if you ask me."

"Think of the young ones, Winnie. The opportunities they'll have."

"I do think of the young ones. But do they ever think about me, I wonder?" Winnie could feel her own voice trembling, along with her knees. She thrust her shoulders forward in an effort to renew her strength. "Am I s'posed to lay down and die now because I'm just an old woman with no reason to live anymore?"

Angela shook her head, her face beginning to redden. "Sure, be as miserable as you want with your own life. But don't you think it's time to set the rest of us free?"

HOLD OUT

Winnie smiled haughtily. "Set yourselves free. I needs me rest."

With those words, Winnie set her body in motion again, edging out the door, supporting herself with one hand against the door jamb as she managed to propel herself into the daylight. The way the sun kissed her face and dazzled her eyes made her think about Francis, how he used to love these days for working in the yard.

"Think about it," Angela called after her, following behind just in case Winnie needed her help. That same bloody beagle barked in the distance as Winnie was crossing the yard. She clamped her hands to her ears until she was safe inside.

She decided the best place to nap would be in her rocking chair that sat in the window, overlooking the yard. From there, she could see the shed, the tall aspens and early-blooming dogwood trees that flourished protectively around it and, in the distance, the beach where the old men stood murmuring to themselves on the dock. The tide being in, the waves rolled forward like markers of time. Later on, when the tide went out, the beach would look dead and smell like a corpse.

She closed her eyes and thought about last night's meeting in the town hall. The whole town had turned out. All thirty-nine souls, including herself. There used to be forty until just two Saturdays ago. But she didn't want to think about that yet. When some things were gone, they were never coming back, and dwelling too much would be harmful.

It was the biggest gathering in years that didn't involve a casket. No one had stayed home because of the prize at stake.

"The government is offering us fifty thousand dollars per household," Mayor Alice Young had announced, her arm stretched high for all to see the brief, typed letter with the government seal.

Her pronouncement had elicited a couple of minutes of excited chatter, some folks in awe and others in doubt.

From her seat in the back of the room, she could only think, *Francis saw this coming.* He should have, since he was the one who'd bargained for it.

"The only catch," the mayor went on, "is that we all have to sign on. That means every last one of us."

That was the part Francis hadn't bargained for all spring. He'd been the one to negotiate with the government, explaining to the minister of rural affairs that the good people of Darwin had pride and a stake in their town, dying or not. They'd spent their lives working and playing, marrying each other, and burying their dead there. The cemetery alone was packed full to its fences with the ghosts of those who had worked to remain here and provide for those who would now leave them behind, though more weeds sprouted on their graves with every passing day.

"No goddamn way," Francis had argued, "that you can uproot these people from their homes for less than a hundred thousand each." He'd blustered his way out of the meeting at the town office that day, sputtering to himself about the heartless baboons who ran the country and wanted everything for nothing. Francis himself had no intentions of leaving, and neither did Winnie. Even then he was dying and they both knew it. He also understood the hardship of trying to start over, but he wanted the best deal possible for those who wanted to go. It was only right.

But fifty thousand was all they would offer. Per household. Even so, they had started at thirty, but Francis had talked them upward.

"No exceptions," Alice Young had said, with a warning in her voice. "There'll be a vote on Monday. And, in the end, every last one of us has to sign the agreement, or they'll have nothing to do with us."

To everyone's amazement, but no one's surprise—since nobody came up that road without everyone knowing who was inside the car—the minister himself stepped to the microphone, made some little speech about being so delighted to

HOLD OUT

visit their wonderful community for the very first time. Then he got to the part that everyone had come to hear. "It's all or nothing," he said. "The premier and I, in consultation with your representatives, have no choice but to recommend that everyone in Darwin vacate the community by August the thirty-first. We simply cannot afford to move half of you away and still support a ghost community of a dozen souls. It's just not economically feasible."

Another murmur chorused through the small crowd. But no one spoke up to disagree. It seemed to be a done deal.

"Now, I know what you're all thinking." The mayor had taken up the microphone again, gently pushing her way in front of the minister, who stepped aside with a slight bow and lowering of the eyes. "We held a vote last year, and there were only two people against the leaving. We all know who that was." All eyes turned to the back of the room, no one speaking, but everyone accusing. Winnie shifted in her seat, feeling the heat of their money-hungry glares. But she was otherwise unmoved and twice as determined.

"Since then, things have changed," said Mayor Young. "Time goes on. We can no longer afford to cling to the past. There's nothing else here for us now. And it's not right that one or two people can force us to stay. We all love our hometown. There'll never be another one like it. And God knows where we'll all go or if we'll ever see each other again. But go we must. And take the money, we will. Otherwise, we leave—or die off—one by one, without any assistance from anyone."

While the officials were speaking, Winnie was pulling on her coat and buttoning it. With the aid of a hand-carved wooden cane, she was able to pull herself up to her feet and shuffle to the door.

Gradually, people had begun to take notice of her and were scrutinizing her, whispering among themselves. Some of them despised her. Others admired her. But they all wished she would change her mind.

Quite unexpectedly, the oldest person in the room stopped in the doorway and turned slowly around to face those who'd been watching her every move. To her aged eyes, the hall looked smaller than she'd ever thought. How many times had she been here for fall fairs or weddings, Saturday night dances, and anniversary parties? *Too many*, she thought, *and yet not enough.* She would love to see at least one more such gathering, where everyone was together instead of apart. *That's what money does to people*, she thought.

She rapped her cane on the door frame, startling the crowd and setting them to murmuring to each other. When she rapped twice more, she had their attention. Everyone, including the mayor, the minister, and the other thirty-seven faces, were all looking at her. She wondered just for a moment what they must think of her. But she decided right then that she didn't particularly care.

"I won't be going anywhere," she said in the loudest voice she could manage. For all her effort, her voice was trembling and weak. Not that she was sick. But she was old, and that carried a certain natural decline.

"It's all of us or none of us," Mayor Young reiterated.

Winnie shook her head. "I'm sorry. But I can't."

When she started to leave, she heard a male voice telling her, "Get back in here!" But she ignored the voice and just kept going.

It was a beautiful night, so she waited outside on the front porch for her ride. She looked up at the stars and thought, *We used to love nights like this, didn't we?* There were some nights she could recall when they'd danced all night; she'd come out for air and stand on the front step while the band struck up a new song, and she hummed to herself. *"Over the Mountain, Across the Sea."* That's what it was, indeed. She was still humming it to herself when the meeting ended, and people were filing outside. Some of them were cordial as they passed on their way to their cars. Others gave her dirty looks, but she didn't mind that. She felt like

107

sticking her tongue out at some of them, but what would that gain her?

Angela Downey practically ignored her as she squeezed past and went to her car, slamming the door behind her. Poor Angela had been a widow for a few years, but she still had her boys living with her, out of work six months of the year, making minimum wage on the government works. Looking through the windshield as Angela started the car, Winnie felt a wave of sympathy nearly move her to tears. *Hard, hard times, as they used to sing.*

"Ready?" Alice Young was the last one out of the hall, but Winnie didn't mind waiting. She was savouring the salt breeze coming off the water.

Alice offered Winnie her arm, which she took, and together they strolled to Alice's car. On the way up the back road along the beach, they talked about what a fair night it was, what a great turnout it had been for the meeting, and how much Francis would have enjoyed it. Twenty years ago, Alice had lived with them when she left her husband for beating her. She'd known Francis well, in fact, for they'd been friends for many years. So even after so much time, she could hold no grudge. After all, once someone's opened up their home to you, you can never rightly begrudge them anything.

They said their goodnights, and Winnie insisted she could walk up the steps by herself. The quarter moon was bright, so there were no worries about seeing her way. She'd be perfectly fine.

"Think about it, is all I ask," Alice had pleaded before Winnie got out of the car.

"My dear," said Winnie with a sigh and patting Alice's hand. "I've thought about hardly anything else lately. You have no idea how much it eats at me."

"It's not just you, you know." When Alice said that, Winnie had to stop and regard her curiously. "None of us wants to leave. No one wants to give up their home."

"Then why are ye doin' it?"

"We don't have a choice, Winnie. You know that."

"Then how come I'm the only one that has to make one?"

She'd left Alice sitting in silence. She'd heard the car turning around in the road and heading back in the direction from which it had come. Alice had honked the horn and Winnie had waved feebly. Then she'd climbed up the steps and opened the door, thankful that she still didn't have to lock it after all these years. The twenty-first century hadn't found her yet, and she'd be damned if she'd let it know where she was hiding. She didn't bother with turning on a light inside, since she knew exactly where she was going.

Winnie wasn't sure how long she'd been asleep in the rocking chair with the purple afghan across her lap when she heard the knock on the door.

It was Angela again, and the morning sun was peeking in through the windows. It pleased her to realize she'd slept through the night.

"It's not that anybody's against anybody." Angela stuck her hands in her apron pockets. "But if we don't all vote the same way, we're gonna lose that money. And none of us can afford to move outta Darwin without that fifty thousand."

Winnie yawned and pulled her blanket snug to her chin. Her home had turned a bit chilly overnight. "There's more to life than money."

"Sure there is. Except when you don't have none, and there's none to look forward to."

"That money will never buy you a new house or a piece of land," said Winnie. "Or peace of mind either."

"Peace of mind?" Angela stood in front of her and crossed her arms. "If that minister leaves here this morning and takes the offer with him, none of us will ever have peace of mind again. Especially you."

With those words, the intruder stomped to the porch and let herself out. Winnie heard the front door slam, just before she closed her eyes and drifted off to sleep again.

HOLD OUT

She awakened again, not knowing what the hell time it was, with the phone ringing. But she let it pass without answering it. Several more times throughout the early morning, it rang, and each time she just let it go until the ringing died away.

"What should I do, Francis, b'y?" She was aware of talking aloud to herself, but she'd been doing it for so many years that she no longer considered it a sign of anything except clarity. Sometimes, the only sensible conversation she had was with herself.

He didn't answer her, but she felt that he was trying to.

"They all wants that money some bad. Not that I blame them. But they don't seem to care about what they're leaving. It's like they don't even know."

She listened again, smacking her lips and suddenly realizing she was thirsty. Throwing off the afghan and leaving it in the chair, she maneuvered to her feet and, after she'd peed in the downstairs toilet, she scuffled to the kitchen for a drink of water. But something made her change her mind. She opened the bottom cupboard, beneath the sink, and pulled out the bottle of Bacardi. "What difference does it make?" she asked and poured herself half a tumbler of rum and took a gentle swallow.

"I know what I should do," she mused aloud. Then a slow smile spread across her face, like the sun rising over the hills. "Francis, you're a genius."

She picked up the phone and called Alice Young to ask for a number.

"You don't need a number," she said. "He's staying here with me."

She told the mayor to put him on and steeled herself for a battle that she didn't think she could win. But nothing was ever won without some kind of effort.

When he came to the phone, she was cordial. He knew who she was. "The hold out," he said with a laugh. "Most popular woman in town, I dare say."

But Winnie had no time for laughing with the likes of him. "Why does it have to be everyone? Why don't you just let me stay here and give everyone their money to go where they please?" *Like a wandering lost tribe of Egypt,* she thought, but kept it to herself. She could practically hear Francis laughing, though.

"I'm sorry," he said. "I don't have the authority. Besides it doesn't make—"

"Economic sense, yes, I know. But there's more sense than money to think about."

"I'm sorry," he offered again.

"Yes, I know." Winnie sighed deeply, feeling her age. The time had come to play her last card. There was nothing else she could do. "Put Alice on the phone."

A few awkward seconds passed before the mayor came on the line.

"Winnie? Is everything all right?"

"Never better, my dear. Just wanted to tell you to go ahead."

"I'm sorry?"

"The moving. The money, and all that. I'm recasting my vote. I'll vote the same as everyone else. You can tell him that before he goes, can you? That'll take care of everything? Good."

She could hear the relief in Alice's voice when she thanked her and asked Winnie if she was sure.

"Sure as anything else in this world."

On the last day of August, dark came early.

Winnie watched the harbour from her seat in the shed. There were no lights on anywhere. The water was silk black, with only a sliver of moon remaining to give shape to the world.

For the first time in decades, nothing was stirring all over town. No pacing men or frowning women. No cars going up or down the road. No screen doors slamming or mowers buzzing.

It wasn't the longest day she could remember, but it was pretty close. Only the afternoon of Francis's funeral had seemed more prolonged and excruciating. She usually lived each moment as it came, but she couldn't do that today. This one wouldn't end soon enough. One by one, from her front porch, she'd watched her neighbours hug and cry, make promises to each other, then get in their overstuffed cars with their rental trailers towed behind, and drive down the road. She watched each one until they were out of sight, and then she would say a silent prayer for them.

A few of them even stopped in to see Winnie and express their gratitude. She would wave them off and say she only did what was right. They would inevitably ask her what she was going to do, but she wouldn't tell them that. "Ask me no questions, I'll tell you no lies" was her safe refrain. Then they would hug her carefully, sometimes kiss her cheek, say thanks once again and be on their way. Every time it happened, Winnie felt happier. It was as if her soul was being slowly lifted towards heaven. Once in while, she found herself humming that song, "Over the Mountain, Across the Sea."

Even Angela Downey had stopped by for a cup of tea. That was the best part for Winnie. When Angela left, Winnie felt for sure she had done the right thing. There were no more hard feelings, no more things left undone. Everyone would get what they needed.

The last car to leave town, just after supper, had been Alice Young's. She stopped and came in for yet another cup of tea, which Winnie poured for her, though she couldn't drink another one herself.

"Why'd you change your mind?" the mayor asked. Winnie was chuffed to see Alice's outfit—a long, black dress with basic white pearls and black shoes. What else would a woman wear on the day her community died? She'd been curious about that, and was grateful that Alice had given her that peek.

"I didn't change my mind about anything."

"But you voted for the money."

"I'll put it to good use, I'm sure. But I never was against the money."

Alice appeared mystified, blowing across the surface of her tea cup. "I don't understand at all."

"You don't have to," said Winnie. "And maybe it's better that way."

A little while later, standing with the car door open, Alice asked, "Is there someone coming for you?"

She thought about it and said, "Don't worry about me. I'll be fine."

But Alice had looked stern then, something in her face threatening to come get Winnie and force her into the car if she had to. "Is there someone coming for you?" she asked again. "Do you have someone who belongs to you?"

"Oh, yes," she said, with a wave to her friend. "We all do, don't we?"

When Alice had left, Winnie took herself out to the shed, to inhale its musty glory and watch the sun go down. She hadn't counted on the moon coming out over the harbour, but that had been a nice touch.

The days would be long now. But the time would be short.

Winnie just sat and stared out the window, marveling at how the moon's reflection made the saltwater shimmer. How many nights had she and Francis sat out here on nights just like this? It had never grown old. They had never tired of each other's company, and the time had never seemed long enough. They had never been rich, but had never wanted anything except to stay like that forever.

She shivered suddenly and thought of an old saying that made her smile.

She arose from the bench and picked up her lamp. Then she made her way slowly to the door and across the yard, marveling at how quiet the world had become.

Somewhere out near the wharf, a lone dog barked. Winnie stopped in her tracks and squinted towards the harbour. There was nothing to see but the moon's ghostly glow upon the water. Nothing to hear but the sift of the ocean seizing the shore and a whisper of wind that made the dogwood leaves tremble.

HOLD OUT

Tomorrow, she would go looking for that dog in the light of day. Something to keep her company on the cold autumn nights.

"I'm home," she said, half jokingly when she stepped inside her front door. Thankfully, the electricity still worked, though for how long, she couldn't guess. It was probably only a matter of days or weeks at the very best.

She didn't bother to turn on a light. There was no sense in that when she knew that house like she knew her own mind.

She eased her way into the living room and, finally relinquishing a soulful sigh, let herself sink slowly into the comfort of her rocking chair. She pulled the purple afghan over herself and gazed out the window at the sliver of moon.

"Goodnight," she said and closed her eyes.

No one answered, but she'd expected that.

Winnie had always prided herself on knowing just what was coming.

THE NIGHT WATCHMAN
MICHAEL CRUMMEY

Darkness wakes me. The moon rises at the tips of my fingers. I stare out the window, watching lights nip out in houses up and down the street. By eleven, the town looks deserted. On the other side of the world, the sun is up. Awake, like me, but with more company.

Sometimes I go upstairs to my bed and watch the ceiling. Sometimes I pull on my boots and walk for hours. I could make my way through town with my eyes closed, circling my stations like a blind horse on its milk route: the mill, the train shed, the core shacks, then down Bennett's Hill to the bunkhouse, past Ellen's old place at the foot of Main Street. I suppose it was those years of shift work, of sleeping through daylight that keeps me up now. For thirty years, I was the night watchman in Black Rock.

Walking the streets of a town at night, you get to see the soft underbelly of people's lives. It was a lonely job. I knew too much about everyone: which couples were up fighting in the middle of the night; who was sneaking from the bunkhouse to meet a married woman, or a girl not yet eighteen, out by the trestle; who stumbled bleary-eyed and hung-over on their way to work just minutes before the whistle blew.

Occasionally, I learned more than I wanted to know and the knowing crawled under my skin and burrowed in there. Maybe it's that remembering makes the night so hard to get through.

***

What needs to be understood is this: when I reported Stick Walker to the Company, I was just doing my job.

I was making my second round of the shift that night, a little before one in the morning. There were lights in the windows of the laundry as I came around Bennett's Hill, which was nothing unusual. The Chinaman was up that late as a rule, often later, working by the light of kerosene lamps, and he'd already stoked the fire for the irons by the time I did my last round at seven a.m. I'd never spoken to him beyond dropping off and picking up my clothes, but I felt I knew him better than most. I waved to him from the street as I walked by and he nodded without looking up from his work. We were each a marker in the other's schedule, as predictable as the Company whistle bracketing shifts.

As I came closer to the building that night, I heard a fuss inside, two voices arguing, a man's drunken laughter, and I began walking more quickly toward the one-storey shack. "C'mon, you fucker," someone was insisting, "have a *dlink* with me, have a fucking *dlink*."

Both men turned guiltily in my direction when I came in, as if I had caught them kissing. They were standing beside one another, and Stick was holding Wah Lee's dark blue shirt at the shoulder. He was almost a foot taller than the Chinaman and he looked like he was scolding a child. The air in the room was thick with steam and the smell of laundry bluing. Shirts and pants hung to dry on clotheslines across the room, like empty skins. When he realized who I was, Stick let go of Wah Lee's shirt. He made a clumsy attempt to push a silver flask into the inside pocket of his coat, but it fell to the floor with a *thunk*. We all stared at it there, lying on its back like a turtle with its belly exposed.

"What's going on here?" I said.

Wah Lee shook his head vigorously. "Mister Stick just leaving," he said. "Good night, good night." He waved with both hands toward the door, shooing us outside, but nobody moved. Stick pulled out a cigarette and lit it, dropping the match to the floor where it burnt down to the end before going out. Finally, I stepped forward and picked up the flask, slipping it into my coat pocket.

"Stick," I told him, "you'd best be getting back to the bunkhouse."

"Me and the Chinaman were just having a chat," Stick said, a mouthful of smoke escaping his lips with each word. "No concern of yours, Mr. Watchman."

"I mean it, Stick," I said.

He raised his hands above his shoulders and nodded his head. "Alright, Mr. Watchman, sir," he said. "Don't have to get upset about this. Nothing to get upset about, is there Chinaman?" He made his way to the door and turned to back through, winking at Wah Lee and myself before stepping outside into darkness.

Wah Lee bent to pick up the black stub of the match from the floor. "Mr. Stick no trouble," he told me. "I don't want no trouble."

"I'll take care of this," I said.

"I don't want no trouble."

"Don't worry about it," I told him, and I left then to make sure Stick was on his way to the bunkhouse.

***

The night watchman's job, as I understood it, was simply to watch and record. "Don't get involved." I was told when I

THE NIGHT WATCHMAN

started. "Keep an eye on things, but stay clear where you can. You don't break up fights or get in the middle of arguments. You're just an observer, understand? See anything out of order, you bring the report to us and we'll take it from there."

Some observations from my first year as night watchman: the sidewalks on Main Street were made of wooden slats, the roads were ankle deep in mud during spring and fall; the Black Rock Miners senior men's hockey team won the Herder Memorial Trophy over the St. John's Capitals for the second year in a row; the Company cut the lights from midnight until seven, leaving power on only for the mills and a sparse crop of streetlamps; Wah Lee's wife arrived from China to live with him in Black Rock late that August.

Trivial details when you set them out bald like that, and separate from one another. I've lived alone all my life for no reason I can single out, although I know some combination of these insignificant details is partially to blame.

No one can remember when Wah Lee came to Black Rock, or how he ended up here. Some say that when he arrived on the train he couldn't manage a single word of English, a piece of paper pinned to his lapel addressing him like a parcel: *Wah Lee, Black Rock by way of Black Rock Jet.* The men in the bunkhouses brought him their work clothes and long underwear, exchanging them for stubs of paper inscribed with a horizontal row of Chinese characters. They kept the ticket on a nail over their beds, having learned that Wah Lee meant business when he said, "No ticked, no crothes." He never smiled, bent over the irons on the stove or the row of steaming wash tubs as soon as he had written your stub or returned your laundry, silently dismissing you.

After his wife arrived from China, Wah Lee seemed to withdraw even further into himself, as if he was going back to his own country in his mind. It was a rare thing to lay eyes on his wife at all; she kept herself hidden away in a room at the back of the laundry. There were a dozen rumours about her making the rounds that year. People said that it cost Wah Le every cent he had to bring her here, that for a while they were reduced to boiling and eating grass because they had no money for food. They said that Mrs. Lee was "not herself" and made life hell for the Chinaman; that she refused to drink or cook with water from the taps, convinced that it was poisoned, and forced Wah Lee to carry buckets down to the brook below their house at six each morning to fetch their daily supply.

Four times a night I walked down Bennett's Hill to clock in at the bunkhouse station, passing Wah Lee's laundry. More often than not I could hear the low wail of a woman's voice from the back room, a wounded sound like something a trapped animal might make. Sometimes I heard Wah Lee's voice as well, speaking his own language or simply cooing as you would to a child, trying to offer some sort of comfort.

Some would claim I had it in for Stick Walker and I won't deny that I was happy to make my report to the foreman. Drunkenness, especially public drunkenness, was frowned upon by the Company. Anyone else would have been shipped out of town on the next train with orders given to officials in the Junction not to allow them beyond that point if they tried to return. But I knew things would be different with Stick.

The Company brought him in from Kirkland Lake, Ontario, to play with the Black Rock Miners. Officially, he was employed in the machine shop, where I worked before taking the job as night watchman. In reality, he was paid to play hockey. Stick showed up when he felt like it and didn't do much when he did. "Kennedy," he'd say to the Shift Boss, limping into the shop two hours late, "I'm not up to work today. Stomach ache," he'd say. Headache. Bad back. Sore shoulder. On his way out the door, he'd wink at the rest of us bent over our machines and then step through into the light of the day.

I knew nothing much would come of my report. A slap on the wrist at most. But in my eyes, that was better than nothing. Less than an hour after I spoke with my foreman that morning, two men were sent to the bunkhouse. They dragged Stick

THE NIGHT WATCHMAN

out of bed, escorted him to the machine shop and put him to work on the grinding stone, sharpening the metal bits for the underground drills. Dog work. Your hands going numb from the vibrations, your eyes watering from staring at the spinning stone.

Fair enough, I thought. It looked good on the smug son of a bitch. My job didn't make me any friends, but occasionally it brought a certain amount of personal satisfaction. I went to the mess hall, where I ate a huge breakfast. Then I went to my bed and slept straight through until suppertime.

***

I suppose something more needs to be said about Ellen; although, it's only in my own head that she's a part of this story at all.

She lived with her parents in a house at the bottom of Main Street. For a short time, I knew the place well, called regularly, shared meals with the family, played Crib and Crazy Eights in the living room. I took her to movies at the theatre on Saturday evenings, to the bowling hall on Wednesdays. I thought I might ask her to marry me one day, and I took the job as night watchman for the raise, began saving for a ring.

From her bedroom window, she looked out over the Company stables and the rail end of Bennett's Hill road leading to the bunkhouses. She waited there each night until I had passed by on my first round, her hand against the darkness of the pane. She may have loved me, I'll never know for sure now. For a long time, I regretted not knowing and wouldn't forgive myself for making the decision I made. Even after she married and moved into her own place, I watched for her at that window. But the farther I move away from it, the more inevitable it seems that things happened the way they did.

All through that winter, Mrs. Lee's illness worsened, as if the foul weather was slowly entering her body, the way it enters the nooks and crannies of a building. On nights the wind was right, her voice carried to the tracks that marked the border of the mill-site. And as I neared the laundry, I heard the sound of Wah Lee's voice as well, babbling helplessly against the current of the woman's panic. Sometimes I stopped outside the shack and considered knocking at the door, but couldn't imagine what help I might offer. Besides, I told myself, it wasn't my job to get involved.

There was heavy wind and sleet that night in February, the only time I laid eyes on her myself. I half ran, half walked along Bennett's Hill, thinking only of reaching the bunkhouses where I could get in out of the weather for fifteen minutes. The noise of the storm was deafening and my head was bowed against the rain. Mrs. Lee almost knocked me down as she ran by in a white cotton nightshirt. Her feet were bare. Her hair was loose around her head. Wah Lee came out the door of the laundry and he grabbed my arm as he went by, pulling me along as he chased after her.

She was a tiny slip of a woman, but it took both of us to cart her inside the laundry and I helped take her to the back room. "*Hala, hala,*" Wah Lee kept repeating, "*Hala.*" There was a single kerosene lamp and I could make out a small bed with an iron frame, a porcelain chamber pot on the floor that needed to be cleaned. We carried his wife to the bed, and Wah Lee fitted a leather harness that was fastened to the bed frame around her shoulders, while I held her. Her nightshirt was soaked through and clung to her body. I could have counted her ribs as she strained against the harness, crying, yelling words I didn't understand. There were raw, bald patches on her head where it looked like the hair had been torn from her scalp. "Prease," Wah Lee said, to me this time. "Prease." He took my arm and led me out into the laundry room, where I leaned against a shelf of washed and ironed clothing. "Wife very sick" he said. "But she okay now, she okay."

"You can't keep her tied up in there like that," I said. "It's not right."

Wah Lee bobbed his head quickly. "No, no, only when wife sick. She safe here," he said. "Prease."

The smell of the chamber pot and the heat of the laundry room made my stomach turn and I hurried out into the sleet, throwing up by the side of the building. Then I walked slowly toward the bunkhouses, glad for the cold rain against my face, letting it soak my head. At the bunkhouses, I woke my foreman and booked off sick for the rest of the night. By morning, I was running a fever so high I couldn't sit up. For three days afterwards, I missed my regular shift.

I never saw Wah Lee's wife again, although I would hear her at times. Her voice from the back of the laundry was like the sound of the ocean inside an empty shell, the sickness coming and going like the tide.

It was a freak accident that ended Stick Walker's hockey career. No one can even say for sure what happened, the best guess being that a spot of blasting powder on the bit he was sharpening was ignited by sparks from the grinding stone. The steel bit exploded in his hand, shards passing through his palm, shattering bones in his wrist and arm.

By the time I made my way to the mess hall for supper that day, the news was making the rounds. No one noticed the spot of blood on his forehead until he was taken to the hospital and the much uglier wounds of the arm had been attended to. Stick reported no pain in his head, only an irritating itch around where the hole had been punctured. An X-ray revealed a metal splinter half an inch long sitting in the frontal lobe of the brain. There was nothing to do, the doctor concluded, but leave it there and hope for the best.

Eventually, the arm healed and he recovered almost full use of his fingers and hand. But Stick had lost his easy way, his cockiness. He was unpredictable, prone to fits of sudden rage and cursing. He couldn't stickhandle a puck or follow the flow of a game. He rarely spoke to the men in the machine shop, kept his distance at the bunkhouse. Even his closest friends before the accident became strangers to him.

He'd walk the streets at night, muttering and swearing under his breath. I'd see him approaching in the distance, drifting through the silver pools of the street lamps. And there were nights I'd come upon him standing outside the laundry, late, after Wah Lee had gone to bed. He paid no attention to me as I eased up beside him. He went on staring in through the windows, swearing quietly. "Fucking chink," he said, "Fucking chink."

I don't' know why he blamed Wah Lee for the change that took place in his life, rather than me. But in his mind, I receded into the background, an innocent bystander in the events leading up to the accident. "Stick," I'd say quietly, placing a hand on this arm. "Stick, you'd best be getting back to the bunkhouse."

On one occasion, I found him pounding with both hands on the door of the laundry. "Come out here," Stick was yelling. "You fucker, come out here!" No one stirred inside and I stood at a distance, ready to step in if I had to. After a few minutes, Stick lost interest in the door and wandered off.

I should have reported him for that, I suppose. I could have written him up, had him sent out of town. But even at its worst, his anger had a lost, aimless feel to it, lighting on one thing for a time, then drifting elsewhere, like a moth mistaking one streetlamp after another for the moon. I never expected anything to come of it, and I'd caused him enough grief already. That was my thinking at the time.

It was late spring; the roads were bogged with mud. There was a good breeze of wind blowing across the townsite toward the mills. I heard the yelling from a long way off and tried to run, but only succeeded in falling repeatedly. By the time I reached the laundry, the two men were locked in each other's arms, as if they were dancing together, drunkenly. They lurched into the oily light of a kerosene lamp on an ironing board, knocking it to the floor. I remember the sound of glass breaking, the roar of flame travelling through spilled fuel, the shelves of cleaned and pressed clothing catching fire. The light in the room flared into brightness, every corner illuminated. I tried to separate the two men, but they wouldn't let go of one another and I had to drag them through the door together. By then, their clothes were burning, too. They fell wrestling to the ground and I rolled them in the mud to douse the fire. "Break it up," I shouted. "Break it up."

Everything stopped when Mrs. Lee began screaming inside. The two men moved away from each other, as if a song in their heads had suddenly finished playing. Wah Lee got to his feet and moved towards the doorway, but the entire laundry was alight and he had to hold his arms up to shield his face from the heat. He shouted into the noise of the fire as it ate its way through the shack, from the inside out. I turned away then and watched Stick walk slowly toward the bunkhouse, as if he had already forgotten what had happened, why his clothes were wet with mud, why his hair smelled burnt.

While my back was turned, the roof collapsed, throwing a shower of sparks at the stars.

China is ten thousand miles from Newfoundland. When I'm walking through darkness, the sun is shining there. Night and day. We used to tell kids around here that if you dug a hole from Black Rock straight through the earth, you'd find yourself in the middle of China, that you'd be standing upside down. Teasing them, you see, although the literal truth of it is, if it was possible to do such a thing, that's where you'd end up.

What I think about sometimes is this: Wah Lee on the Company train in his blue pajama suit and pig tail, not a word of English in his head, chugging toward Black Rock with that label pinned to his chest. Who addressed him like a letter and put him on the train? A little man coming along into a place of strangers, his life turned upside down.

After the fire burned down to embers and most of the people who had come out of their houses in long underwear and boots went home, I headed down Bennett's Hill road to the bunkhouse to clock in. I was in shock, I guess. I looked up at Ellen's window as I went by, but she had given up waiting. And it occurred to me that we were strangers, that I had no idea what it would mean to be married to her.

This was a long time ago, of course. No one remembers much about it anymore, besides myself, and I've long since given up trying to answer the old questions, though they're still with me. Was she strapped in her leather harness when the fire took her? Did she choose to stay there? Am I to blame for all of this? For a time, there was nothing I wanted more than to know the answer to these things. But now, I think the best I can do is simply to say as clearly as I can, "This is what happened. These are the things I saw."

There's no hint of the laundry's foundation in the ground now. The laundry tubs and ironing boards, the bed with the iron frame, the chamber pot, all of it gone, lost in the darkness. There's just myself now to say what stood here, what happened in this place. And someday soon, I know, I'll be lost in the darkness as well.

HER ADOLESCENCE

SARA TILLEY

Eva is tired, she's been tired since she woke up, she's been tired since before that, since last year, and who knows, maybe even since before then. She has dark circles under her eyes which, when she catches a sidelong glance of herself in the mirror, she thinks make her look dead, already. A spook. She feels dead. Although supposedly once you pass over, there's some rest.

Eva doesn't rest anymore, she barely remembers the sensation. She is in constant motion, even in sleep. Mabel's strange sentences swirl through her dreams, often to the tune of "There Is Power In The Blood", or one of the other hymns they used to sing in school. She tosses and turns with her jaw clenched tight, fighting off the words all night, waking with a headache that starts in the fibrous knotty muscles in her jaw, spreading upwards through her ears into her temples. Coming awake with the words still faintly there, in the background, wafting away on faint tendrils of imagined music: there's wonderful power in the Blood. This morning when she woke she

127

HER ADOLESCENCE

had to pull at her jaw to get it open, massaging around the lump of muscle in her cheek, clenched so tight it felt like bone. For several seconds there was nothing but the cool morning air on her bare feet, and the circular motion of her fingers on her jaw, and the sound of Mary, still asleep, and the view out the window: the wind lapping up peaks of water into frothy white mountaintops, and the gulls dipping in and out of the valleys, fishing for their breakfasts. For a minute or so she was content, by herself, trying to remember the words from her dream, content to stand and strain her mind toward remembering, as though there was nothing more to life than that. Then the last traces of music left her, and she was once again forced to acknowledge that this was not simply a sunny morning with a nip in the air, but that her mother was ill, she was very ill, she was getting worse daily, and it fell to Eva to replace her. Eva's shoulders dropped a little, and she clenched her jaw tighter. She held her spine straight and prepared to get through the obligatory morning chores. This was her life; it was a life of service.

She drank her requisite two glasses of water from the bedside pitcher, and dressed in her work skirt and blouse with the elbows nearly gone. It was a chilly morning with a premonition of fall, so she put her woollen stockings on, and pinned her hair back as tightly as she could, which was not very tightly, as she had never worn her hair any way but loose and long or in a braid until last year, when she had turned thirteen. Now Eva always wore her hair in a knot, with any stray strands secured with small metal pins. Her mother had told her how to do this and then made her write it all down in her notebook, as Mrs. Tilly was the schoolteacher and used to giving dictation. Now that she was ill, she was determined to continue in this fashion, leaving behind a record of necessary information that Eva could look to when she was in need of guidance, afterwards.

River water is most impure and still water is unfit for dish washing or Cooking   still water always causes fever   every healthy person requires 2 to 4 pints daily   Bathing is the most important thing in life do not Bathe an hour before or after any meal

The proper way to wash dishes are: first you collect all the dishes cups first, then saucers, then spoons, then knives and forks, and small plates, lastly large plates   all in separate heaps   Then remove cloth and get a pan of hot soapy water. Wash cups and saucers first, knives and forks next, then small plates, lastly all your large plates. Then get another pan of hot water and rinse them all over the same order then dry with a clean towel or leave them on a rack to dry.

Of course Eva already knew how to do dishes, although left to her own she would not have executed the task in such an exacting and scientific manner. In the past year she has dedicated most of her time to caring for four things: her mother, the young ones, the house, and Duke. She has taken down nearly a full notebook's worth of dictations from her mother, about ninety pages, although some of these are occupied with other, secretive writings: about Walter, or else occult in nature, or else her draft letter to the girl in the Yukon, Miss Flora E. Middlecoff Mayo, whose father knew Duke when he was a young man and out in the wide world, up in the wild country he sometimes gives talks at church about. *Life on the Alaskan Frontier.* Eva tilts the book away from her mother as she writes. She has learned how to perform all household chores with efficiency on a strict weekly, daily, or hourly schedule—the schedule is written out so she doesn't forget. She has disinfected, dressed, washed and massaged her mother. She has combed her mother's hair and washed it. She has helped her void her bowels, she has cut her toenails and tended to her sores. She has given her a cleaning with lukewarm water every day, using a flannel sheet to cover all but the part being softly washed with a cloth and quickly patted dry. The sheet, the cloth, the bowl, all boiled in carbolic acid when she's done, as are the numerous rags. Eva has had to cut up two whole bed sheets for rags, as her mother's cough has grown worse in recent weeks. There are two bowls, one for clean rags and one for bloody, and last thing at night Eva boils down the bloody ones, her

HER ADOLESCENCE

smock and mask still on. Then her sickroom clothes are also washed in carbolic and hung over the woodstove.

For Duke, she's just cooked, washed, and kept quiet. He's at home as little as possible. He's got work to do and is caught up with the new political man, or is at least using that as an excuse to come home long past suppertime, on most evenings. Eva remembers way back to when she was Robert's age and Duke would let her ride him around the yard like a pony while she helped him pick potatoes. Now she absents herself as much as possible when he's around. When they do eat together, they barely say anything. Eva has learned to read Duke's hand gestures for "fetch more bread" or "pass the salt". She has the babies eat in the kitchen as Duke can't tolerate their voices, and they are too small to stop their chatter when it's prudent. They can't read the storm clouds gathering behind their father's eyes, not like Eva can. He seems to be growing his whiskers out longer these days. The children at school used to call him Mad Man Tilly. They said he was half insane and if he caught you on his property he'd skin you and tan you and make himself a coat—or a vest, if you were on the scrawny side.

Mustard poultice for adults

1 part mustard to 4 parts Flour   Make into paste with luke-warm water. Hot water if used will destroy the quality of mustard. Spread over half cloth then turn other half over. Fold corners. Do not keep on for longer than 15 or 20 minutes.

Now that her mother was too sick to teach, there was no school. For the first four months of her illness, Mrs. Tilly had continued to grade assignments and set lesson plans. Now she doesn't have the energy, and has abandoned the school altogether. Mrs. Tilly knew she would not recover, she could feel the illness inside her lungs, wet and spongy, glutting itself on the oxygen she struggled to drag inside. She didn't tell Eva this, nor did she request a visit with her other children. She kept her opinions on her imminent death to herself and continued to maintain her teacherly demeanour, even as her eldest daughter tended to her as you would a newborn. Mrs. Tilly dictated the rules for tooth-brushing, bed-making, for the cleaning of sores. How to make baked apples, and coffee for Duke, and rhubarb water with lemon, and cream toast where you toasted bread and dunked it in warm milk with salt. Eva would sit in the sick room chair and write down all she could, as her mother spelled out the ways in which a woman was supposed to keep a house together, keep everyone nourished, and clean, and comfortable, how a woman had to work very specifically, on behalf of all those in her care, to fight grime, vitamin deficiency, and sloth.

For her mother's birthday, Eva made a feast, consisting of all the recipes she'd been dictated so far.

5 dishes

Mutton broth, fruit jelly, milk pudding, hot water toast, and hot drink

She had never made milk pudding before and burned it, but her mother ate some anyway, and said it was a good first try, although not a passing grade. Eva was stung by this, but knew her mother would never grade you higher than what you deserved, especially if you were her daughter. She was a strict teacher with high standards for all of her students, but because she expected so much, her praise, when won, warmed you through to your bones. That day she tasted everything and even had a half a bowl of the broth, which Eva thought a bit too fresh, but her mother said that in recent weeks she'd an aversion to salt and it was perfect. When she was taking the leftover food out, Eva disobeyed her mother's very first dictation about caring for a sick patient and did not discard the remainder lest someone else be contaminated from contact with it. No, she did the opposite, the dangerous, she ate up the broth—the perfect broth!—from the bottom of her mother's bowl, tried to feel it in her mouth as it would have felt in her mother's mouth, soothing her, pleasing her, giving her a minute of contentment amid the long, strained days and weeks and months that she'd been in the sick room. *Long journey   lady fading   sad lady wastes in grey   she is up high in the*

HER ADOLESCENCE

air and we see her disappear there is no starlight and no lamplight for thirty days. In a way, Eva wanted to contract the illness too, as she didn't want to think about what it would be like later, once the inevitable happened and it was just her and Duke and the little ones here, and him really taking to the role of Mad Man Tilly, setting fires in the woods and never changing his clothes, forgetting to eat or to bathe, drinking himself into unconsciousness. Mary and Robert clinging to her legs like burrs, weighing her down, wailing with grief. Hungry, dirty, in need of her.

She wanted to be close to her mother, closer than her mother's rules allowed. The caregiver is not to have excessive physical contact with the patient or to breathe too closely to the patient's face. Eva has special gloves she has to wear. She keeps them in the pocket of her sickroom smock, which hangs outside the sickroom door, and is long enough to cover all of her clothes. She also has a cloth mask to put over her mouth. It makes her feel like she is hiding, and in a way she's glad her mother can never see her full expression. Eva doesn't think the smock or mask have much effect, but her mother is very strict about maintaining as much of a quarantine situation as possible. Duke and the children are not allowed inside the room, as it is important to maintain consistency: one person with the utmost standards of hygiene should be the sole caregiver of the patient, and Duke is a fisherman, a farmer, a trapper and a logger, so hygiene is not on the top of his priority list. He has work to do and food to be procuring for Eva's rudimentary preparations, and besides which, he's become strained and awkward with Mrs. Tilly since her illness started, as though he doesn't recognize his own wife anymore. He'd never been one for making small talk with strangers.

So, throughout the spring and now the summer new rhythms were established, which, strange and topsy-turvy at first, soon transformed into the unacknowledged everyday motion of their lives. Eva left off everything she used to do for herself, which wasn't too much. Her Sunday group. Practicing on the church piano. Walking in the woods with Walter. Stealing up to Bird Island Cove to see Mabel, against her mother's say-so.

She'd been foolish for Walter, recently even, foolish for that eerie feeling on the back of her neck. Ever since she had turned thirteen in April they'd been going up back of the farm together. He'd touched her bubs before they'd even started to show, and hadn't let on any disappointment. That wasn't long ago. They had been picking blackberries. They had a secret spot they liked to go, out back of the farm where the land was still the same as when people had first arrived here. The blackberry bushes went up past your eyes and were full of vicious thorns, but Eva knew a spot where there was a bush you could push through into a little clearing, almost perfectly round, with berries on all sides. About big enough for two people, if they were friendly with one another. Duke had showed it to her long ago, he called it a Charmed Circle. Supposedly if you stayed in there too long, the Little People would catch you in their snares. It was a story his father had told him when he was her age. Duke knew all the secrets about the family land. When Eva was a girl, they would pick berries together and he'd dare her to go pick by herself in the circle, and she never would, because she always half believed his stories. He had a serious expression when he spoke.

That day with Walter, back in July, the bucket was not very full, and what was there was carelessly picked, as they were only half paying attention, more intent on nuzzling each other. His breath was hot and sweet and his tongue and teeth were purple with berry juice. They had been kissing for weeks now, but this was the first day she felt his hands on her, burrowing their way into her clothes.

I wish I were an old boot
And you a piece of leather
And some kind friend would come along
And nail us both together
If my heart were a head of cabbage

HER ADOLESCENCE

That grew and split in two
The leaves I'd give to others
But the heart I'd keep for you

She'd written those before the notebook had been taken over with instructions on how to lead a clean existence with little chance of contracting a fatal disease. There were a lot more poems than that, at least ten pages worth, at the front of the book. Near the back were her notes from the visits to Mabel. *Sad at heart   red bastard   no words but the lips will betray you   some girl but she looks like a sheep   white cream girl   him hands like wasp stingers.* That day, after he'd touched her and she'd backed away in shock and then relented and kissed him on the mouth, she'd let Walter see the front of the notebook, to make up for things. He'd laughed at her, but there was something shy in his eyes too. And then maybe some fear as she took out her pencil, turned to a new page, and wrote out her own set of instructions for living.

Ten Commandments of Love
Remember thy beloved sweetheart
Thou shalt not make goo-goo eyes at any other girl
Thou shalt not wink at any other girl
Thou shalt not love to kiss but kiss to love
Thou shalt not be to thy sweetheart a penalty
Thou shalt not do anything in private that thou would not do in public
Thou shalt not love two when one will do
Thou shalt not ask for a kiss but take one
Always kiss a girl when she refuses for she does not like to say yes
Whosoever reads the ten commandments of love must pay the penalty asked. If he refuses take him away from me.

Walter said Eva was contradicting herself with these so-called rules. Eva said that she regretted letting him touch her there, and didn't think it was proper, as she was only thirteen, after all. Walter said that was hypocritical as she'd just shown him her love poems, hadn't she? Eva wanted to know why love always had to be about the body. Why couldn't he just love her in the way she wanted him to? He asked for a kiss and she refused so he forced one from her, as per commandments eight and nine. She protested more and he kissed her harder. He touched her on the bubs and she said no, don't do that, and he said back that he knew that she wanted him to. They spilled the bucket of berries when he pushed her down onto the grass and she kicked out in surprise at his weight on top of her. What's the penalty I must pay for having read your rules? said Walter. Then Eva began to cry and he felt very sorry. He pushed out through the thorns and got water from the brook to wash her face with. Walter told her that he loved her and that although they were very young he was sure this was forever. If she wanted it, he would ask her father about proper courtship, even though he did think Mr. Tilly was a dirty Smallwood man. She said she liked the secret of being with him, and that it was their special thing here in the circle. He joked about the Good Folk bewitching them some night, leading them astray into the Good Kingdom, until they lost their minds and turned into animals, naked on all fours in amongst the trees. Eva meowed like a cat and Walter pounced on her, and kissed her, and she said no, don't, so he did it some more. She pried herself out from under him and got up, scrubbing at the blackberry stains which were blooming deep purple and red all over her skirt. Walter seemed unable to stand.

You always disappoint me.

What does that mean, Walter? I showed you my book, I told you things, you kissed me, and now I have to go as Mother needs her tea.

You always pick your mother over me, Eva.

What an evil thing to say, you bastard boy.

I don't care if it's evil, it's the truth.

Don't be a sook. She bent and kissed him and said she loved him but couldn't he understand her mother was sick, she couldn't fix her own tea anymore, she couldn't do anything, she needed help to sit up, to do her toilet, she couldn't do anything anymore, you understand? Walter said he

HER ADOLESCENCE

understood, but Eva didn't believe him, and ever since then they'd only gone picking once and he hadn't tried anything much, and had avoided her eyes, looking like someone had kicked him.

When you're ready to be sweet you come and find me.

Thinking of Walter made Eva think of berry picking, which made her think of the blueberries which grew up in the meadow, and which were now ripe, which made her think of her mother, who loved blueberry buckle more than any other dish. Back when she was well, Mrs. Tilly used to talk about making the first pan of it all summer, walking up to the back of the land every morning to check for early ripe ones, once August hit and the berries started going from white-green to pink to blue. Eva had the recipe, although she hadn't tried it yet. As she washed the young one's clothes and did the floors, she thought of her mother's face, pleased and proud. Even if she couldn't eat it, the smell alone would do her good. After reading, and sums, and lunch, she sent the young ones across the road to play and headed up to the back of the land with her bucket. Her mother was sleeping well, and wouldn't need her till at least four o'clock. Eva swung the bucket happily. She started up past the blackberry patch, picked bare long ago, and then she stopped. There was a sound. At first she thought it was partridge, or something. Rustling. But then there was this kind of moan, like someone was hurt, and then another, and then a giggle, and then she headed straight into the blackberry circle with her bucket held in front of her, a shield for the thorns. They looked like a painting, having frozen in place when they heard her charging in on top of them, nearly falling right on top of them as the circle was so small. For a second no one spoke, nothing moved save the blackflies. Eva felt herself grow flushed. She had been warned. *White as cream red hand boy fragile girl is turning to marble.* There in their spot, in her charmed circle, where he had kissed her neck and felt underneath her clothes and said he wanted to marry her. It was on Duke's property. It was a place only she would go, or Duke himself, and Walter would have known that, and chosen the place purposefully, maybe hoping for Eva to interrupt them, or else her father, who knows. When she crashed through the bush on top of him and Gertie Hancock his face didn't look any redder than usual. His hands did, though. Seemed once a boy turned fourteen he just couldn't live for a week without grabbing hold of some girl's bubbies. Gertie Hancock's flabby bubs. She'd been the most well-developed girl in school, back when they had school. Gertie had lumps at nine, and a womanly shelf at eleven. Eva had always thought it was embarrassing, but obviously Walter thought otherwise. He didn't look sorry at all.

You bastard, bastard boy.

Eva, girl, you drove me to it. No satisfaction for a month.

Gertie started crying, scrambling to do up the front of her dress, wiping her face with her hem, trying to stand. Don't tell my father, will ya?

You can both fly to hell. She could hear Mabel's words circling around louder and louder inside her head. *Betrayed by flesh   hands you know on strange snow   skin like cold soft shame   thorny bush all around the circle.* Eva threw her empty bucket, and though she meant to hit Walter it glanced off Gertie's shoulder and she started crying even louder.

Sorry Gertie. Walter, you can burn to blazes for all I care. Get off Duke's land before I call him up here with his buckshot.

Eva left the bucket, pushed roughly through the bush and walked back toward the house, stopping at the root cellar to pull out a few potatoes to boil with milk toast, for supper. There would be no blueberry buckle tonight. She had scratches starting to sprout bright beads of blood on her arms and neck from her quick retreat through the thorns. She'd never pick in the circle again. The blackberries could rot off their branches and ferment on the ground, she wouldn't care about the waste. The berries could all ferment into wine, get the squirrels drunk, she'd leave them for the Good Folk. Her blood had gone cold, and slow. She dropped the potatoes into her pockets, and

HER ADOLESCENCE

thought better of going inside. Her mother didn't expect her for an hour, and Mary and Robert were still across the road. There was an acid fire inside of her, the shape and size of bastard Walter's bastard hands. She was enraged. She felt numb. She might cry. A walk would help. If she went quickly she could get up to the cove and back again before doing supper. She set off up the road, half-skipping, the potatoes thudding heavily into her thighs.

Mabel, are you having your supper or what? Eva is knocking on the door off the kitchen. Mabel is rarely found anywhere else.

Get yourself inside, I just made jam.

If it's blackberry, no thanks.

Mabel comes to the door, her face red from the stove. Don't tell me it already happened. Who was it?

Gertie Hancock.

Gertie Hancock. And what happened to your arms, my girl?

Mabel has work trousers on, like Duke's, and Eva knows this is part of the reason why her mother does not approve of her. Well, there are other reasons, too, but Eva privately disagrees with Mrs. Tilly on those. Mabel knows things, Mabel sees things. Tea leaves, cards. Once, down on the beach, Eva saw her just receive the voices straight. Mabel. Her hair long and grey, sharply parted in the middle, combed straight and left unbound, so that it falls like a gloomy waterfall right down to the seat of her trousers. Mabel told her two months ago that she foresaw infidelity, another woman, she even pinpointed the location, she said *berry bush circle hidden private yours*. That's the kind of speech she had when she was reading leaves. Who and when had been a mystery. Mabel spoons some raspberry jam onto a thick slice of bread for Eva, gets her a cloth to wash her scratches, and puts the kettle on. Mabel's jam has won prizes at the Bird Island Cove Fair, and perhaps this is another reason why Eva's mother does not like her very much.

The cup she reads from is an ordinary one, a white teacup, just like the plain kind Eva's family uses when there's no company in. It's not the cup, it's the leaves. Eva is glad for her daily dictations, as she can easily copy everything down. When Mabel starts to speak the leaves, she doesn't stop. It all comes pouring out.

Long journey   cross water
A long dress and a pair of high heeled shoes
See a flag half masted   see a strange fellow walk with him on top of cup good luck   get my wish   long long journey see flag half masted

Visitor. Box. A long, long way from home, removal past wonderful. Grey lady turns to dust. Boat. Strange message. Good prospects. Journey across water. I walk with strange man in new shoes. Man unpacking bottles. Lady is air now and lady will vanish. Dishes. Book. Give me journey. See flag half masted. Play the church organ. All the flowers cut down they go into the hole. Get wish. Lady floating into a million lights. I am laughing on a boat. The flowers in the hole are dying. I am laughing the babies are crying   so much noise father has no face. I am going across water big laughing big breathing no one who knows me is there. Time going still again like playing going to sleep.

Eva stands up abruptly and puts her hand over the cup. Stop. Stop please, that's enough.

Mabel blinks. She's back in the room. Anything?

The same as before, a journey and a book. Me getting my wish.

Well, that's good.

Eva puts back on her coat. I'm going to be late. She darts out the door before Mabel can see the guilty tears starting to form in the corners of her eyes, as she allows herself, for once, to luxuriate in the forbidden thought of her mother's death, and to long for it. Death, black death, sitting on her mother's shoulder, lips to her lips, sucking the last bit of her colour away. Mother cold, gone, in the ground. A boat, a journey, a place where she's a stranger. The children taken in by relatives.

HER ADOLESCENCE

Eva wipes her eyes and begins to run, pounding dust up in a long trail down the road towards home. There are sheets to soak in carbolic, rag bowls to empty, poultices to change. She is grateful for the coat, for once—the scratches are hidden from sight. The mask smells clean and scrubbed, she finds it comforts her to put it on, to close off as much of herself as possible under sterilized cloth, boiled in acid until nothing can live on it. She enters the sick room. The remains of her mother's face look up at her, sinking further and further back into the starched pillows, cheeks turning in on themselves, becoming hollow pits, grey and moist. She's barely moving now, and will not take more than a mouthful or two of cream toast for supper tonight, Eva is sure. She clenches her jaw behind her mask, and gently brushes out her mother's hair. She softly wipes her mother's face with a warm damp cloth, but Mrs. Tilly doesn't want a full bath tonight, she doesn't have the energy. Eva wipes down her pencil and the covers of her notebook in carbolic solution before opening it. She sits, ready to copy down any instructions her mother might be able to impart before six o'clock, when she generally grows too tired to speak, and asks that Eva please read to her, or sing one of the old hymns that long ago when she had been a schoolteacher, she'd taught the children of Elliston to sing, gathered around the church piano.

AT SEA

DON ROY

Jesus, he was sick; four days below, paralysed in a bunk as the old trawler pounded into the waves of a nor'easter that seemed to have dropped anchor on the Grand Banks. They came down to get him, "Can you steer?" tired of carrying his load on four-hour watches.

He nodded; had to; told them he'd worked the boats before, when he came looking for a job. "Keep her straight into the waves," the captain's instructions, greying stubble poking through the skin of his windburned face and carpeting the sides and back of his weaving head as he staggered to his quarters at the rear of the wheelhouse. "I just need a few hours."

He had squirreled away half a quart of rum in a crevice on the far side of the dock before he strode up the rusty gangplank, the first half of the bottle still warm in his throat and gut. An hour later, as he stood on deck bathing in cool autumn breezes, the glow still with him, watching Mulgrave get smaller, he wondered why he had waited until now, when he was almost fifty, to adopt this wonderful life on the sea.

AT SEA

But now the comfort of the rum was long gone and he wished for the half bottle he had stashed on shore to celebrate his return. That first night he had dropped into the bunk, stomach full, craving sleep. The alcohol had since washed through, leaving him on his own. During the night, the storm slipped in over them. When they woke him, long before daylight had to compete with the blackness of the clouds flying close to the whitecaps, his hands were trembling and the boiled dinner from supper had gone sour inside him. Even in the bunkroom below waterline, he could hear the shrillness of the wind, complaining as it tore itself open in the rigging. He lurched to the head and filled the grimy toilet with the mash left from the night's meal. Then he slid down to the floor, his back against the cold steel of the hull, and breathed heavily. And when the smell of piss and old fish guts and diesel mixed in his mouth, he puked again until he thought he was empty, and then, again.

The Newfoundlander who lived below deck, married to the diesels and generators, looked him over and sent him back to his bunk. "We be dancing with the sea for a few days me son; you'll be missing the land." And he was right, never before had he been this sick, not even in the first days of detox, when his trembling hands would shake coffee out of the cup before he could drink it. Now, lying in the bunk, he wondered why life was dealing him this hand. If he could have just one drink from that bottle—to wash out his mouth.

It had started good, a lifetime ago: cutting wood with his father, bent over with the bucksaw, young muscles showing off, lunch breaks and stories, following the horse home. Winning Shelia and screwing naked on the covers, oblivious to the snow blowing in around the window of the old shack, her heels dug into the crooks of his knees.

The new pulp mill opened at the Strait and he bought a power saw. Money started rolling in. One Friday afternoon, he drove the old truck, with its homemade wood box, into town, parked in front of the credit union and left for home an hour later in a new convertible. He picked up Shelia, and they drove up and down Main Street until after dark. All summer they cruised, top down, eating fried chicken from the new take-out.

Not long after Christmas, Jilly was born and Shelia stayed home with the blues, well into spring. The snow got too deep to work at the woods so he stayed home, for a while, but he was tired of listening to Shelia and the baby—both crying. He had enough of them and went into town, to the tavern, got drunk and made some new friends. In the beginning, it was only Saturday nights, but as the winter dragged on, he would take the unemployment cheque out of the mailbox, buy a few groceries and some baby food, to keep Shelia off his back, then party until the rest was gone.

The time between cheques felt longer and longer in the little house. He started to stash a bottle in the woodpile to take the bite off the days, and when winter broke and he went back to the woods, he kept a pint in his lunch tin to soften the monotony.

One dull early-summer morning, he found his income tax refund in the mailbox. Instead of going to work, he went into town, cashed it and bought a good stroller so Shelia and Jilly could get out without having to bother him. Then he loaded the car with some of the boys from the tavern and they lit out for Halifax. Two days of hard drinking in the company of thirty-five-dollar whores, the money was spent. A fisherman from the South Shore bought the car, for half of what it was worth, and a week later, he stumbled off the train in Antigonish and hitchhiked the rest of the way home.

The trip cost him his job. He shrugged it off and went to work for another pulp contractor. Lost that one too—and the next one, and then no one would take him on. He got on the system, government grants—cutting brush on the roadsides, just enough weeks to qualify for unemployment.

Just as winter was coming on again, Shelia bundled Jilly in a blanket, snuggled her in the stroller, walked up to the highway and stood waiting for the kindness of a drive, her face red in the coolness of the day. Later she climbed out of a pick-up truck, on its way east, took the stroller out of the back, loaded the groceries she had bought with the welfare chit in around her sleeping daughter and pushed her the two miles home, tears falling against her coat all the way.

No longer would she admit him, drunk and pleading, nor sober and demanding, to her bed. He moved to the couch. As winter slipped back over the land, catching a ride home from the tavern and then wedging himself onto the cushions became less appealing. He took a room in town, down near the tracks—and he never left.

For a few years, he would show up at the door around birthdays and around Christmas with a gift for Jilly. Over time, the gifts became less expensive, less frequent, and then they did not come at all. Visits evolved into chance encounters on the street or at the mall. He would crouch down, put a big hand on her trembling shoulder, smile into her nervous face and remind her who he was, while Shelia stood, thin lipped and fidgeting.

When Jilly was eight, Shelia gave up, tucked her daughter into bed, kissed her goodnight, and took all her pills. Jilly found her in the morning. As they sank her into the earth, he stood across the grave watching his daughter's pale emotionless face, her hand held by the woman from social services, and he wondered how this would affect his life.

Standing at the wheel, ten years later, his stomach pitching with the deck, all that seemed a long time ago. He started to sip the warm soup passed to him in a big tin mug. It tasted wonderful, though he would have traded it for that half bottle waiting on the wharf in Mulgrave in an instant. The muscles in his legs started to find their strength as he swayed fore and aft with the ship as it ploughed through the relentless waves, one hand steady on the wheel, the other holding the cup, floating in the air.

ROY

They'd done a poor job with Jilly, in the foster homes. She quit school. He'd seen her in town, hanging around with losers, crossing the street if she saw him coming—her own father. No big surprise when she started to show. The boyfriend was gone then. He could have told her that was coming. But then a month ago, everything changed. They met unexpectedly on the corner of College and Main, standing together on the same slab of sidewalk, her little stroller at his feet. He bent down and introduced himself to the baby, his granddaughter, looking up with worried eyes—Shelia's eyes. Jilly made small talk on that ripe day of late summer, nervously rocking the light canvas carriage on its small plastic wheels, her puffy body swelling out of her clothing like bread dough rising in a bowl on the back of a wood stove. She invited him to supper at her little apartment and, later that week, he took her up on the offer. They sat on folding chairs at a card table covered with a plastic cloth and, after the baby was asleep in the bassinet in her room, he answered her questions about her mother, as best he could remember. When the rum he had sipped on while walking to her place had worn off, and he became uncomfortable with the directness of her talk, he excused himself, walked to the tavern, sat in his chair and wondered if perhaps they could still make something of what was left of the life fate had dealt them.

It was too soon for the soup, his stomach rejected it, gushing it up his throat. He desperately scanned the wheelhouse for a bucket—anything. There was nothing. He raced to the port door, threw it open and spewed warm vomit over the side. But, when he abandoned the wheel, the gale winds pushed the bow of the trawler to port and the ship rode up and over the wave at an angle and the next wave glanced along her side pushing her over sharply. The captain's door flew open and he raced to the wheel and spun it to starboard, his wool socks sliding on the steep pitched floor. It was too late; the ship slid into the trough almost parallel to the wave towering over it. When it slammed into them, punching out the starboard windows, they rolled to port and put the railings in the sea. The Newfoundlander scurried up out of the engine room and cried out, "Merciful Mary, forgive my sins," and the captain clung to the wheel and roared at the sea, for they both knew that the boat was lost. But Mary did not want them—not yet. As the wave slid away from under them, they started to right and the rudder bit into the sea so that they were swinging back to starboard as they climbed the next wave, still leaning hard to port. Two more waves and she was back on course, the wind blasting through the open windows, chilling the wheelhouse as the two men stared him back to his bunk. A week later when they made Mulgrave, holds half full of fish, the crew climbed into a taxi and left him on the wharf, alone, and broke.

He watched as the car rounded a curve and disappeared. Thankful for the privacy, he walked briskly, the rigidity of the concrete dock an odd sensation, to where he had left his bottle. It was gone. He thrust his arm into the crevice and felt around wildly. *Gone! Stolen! Fucking rummies!* He sank onto his haunches, the sun dropping away from him behind the hills, and he wondered if Jilly might have any money.

EVERYTHING WAS LOST IN THE FIRE

CRAIG FRANCIS POWER

Everything was lost in the fire. And where were you? You were at work, I think. At the café when you got the news about it. It was all over the radio. A whole block of apartments on Gottingen Street burning to the ground, including my place. What we used to call our place back in the days when we were still in love.

It was February. The fire department blocked off the streets all around the apartment. I remember looking up at the telephone wires, and how they had become covered in ice from the water from the fire hoses. Icicles about two feet long hanging down, making the wires dip dramatically in the middle. Someone had brought me the cat. I was crying and worried about him, but a fireman had found him somewhere and someone told him it was mine. I was standing there on the sidewalk with everyone else, little cat in my arms, one blanket around my shoulders, another around him.

That cat, remember him? You saw someone's ad at the corner store. We had talked about getting one only the day

EVERYTHING WAS LOST IN THE FIRE

before. When you came home with the ad we decided it was meant to be. "It's fate," you said. We walked over to the address on the ad and picked him out of the box. He was all black with one small patch, bright as a dime on the top of his head. "Like a halo," you said. We called him Luke. Around that time, you called me Little Devil. "Let's go out to the bar, Devil," you'd say, like the two characters from your favourite Hemingway novel. We used to drink all night back then, and we were hardly fighting at all once Luke was in the house with us. He was good luck, you'd say. Those were the good times, weren't they? Sometimes I think you were the best friend I ever had in my life, but I don't like to think much about it now.

Luke would always be disappearing on us. That kept up even after you moved out. He'd come back skinny as a rail, with a bit of fur missing from fights or whatever trouble he may have gotten himself into. One time he came home through a window, and I saw that his ear had been sliced right down the middle. He was bleeding everywhere. I fixed him up as best I could, but how easy do you think that was? I had red scratches on my arms for days and days. I'd hear all the neighbourhood cats through the bedroom window at night, hissing and yowling so horribly they sometimes sounded like babies crying. Or little girls howling. I'd close my eyes and try to pick out which voice might be his. Trying to figure out if he was okay by the sound of his voice. I admit it's silly to think of a cat as having a voice, but that's what I did a lot of the time at night in our old bedroom, trying to get to sleep.

I'd leave a can of opened tuna on the kitchen table by the open window, sometimes. In the morning all the food would be gone, but there'd be no sign of him. I was probably feeding all the cats on the street trying to get him to come back, but if he came in, he didn't stick around for very long. Sometimes he'd stay, though, and it may be stupid to say but when I'd feel his little feet on the bed, it was the best night of sleep ever. He'd start purring and I'd scratch his head and say

POWER

"Hi Lukey. Welcome home Lukey." and he'd settle down onto the covers and close his eyes.

From the sidewalk, I watched the wall with all my books on the bookshelf cave in. I could see it right through the window. The room was bright because of the flames so I could even make out a couple of old pictures on the wall. The crowd of people who had gathered around to watch would ooh and aah like they were watching fireworks going off. There were some strangers around me who did their best to comfort me. Getting me hot tea from their house, or another blanket or whatever I needed because they felt so bad for me. Luke was trembling in my arms. The blanket wasn't really doing much good, but he seemed to not want to run off somewhere. He seemed content in my arms despite the cold. Like he knew something terrible was happening to us, and wanted to stay with me.

You could be really awful sometimes. You probably don't remember that much about it. You'd drink sometimes from noon until noon again. Even while we were living together, there were times you'd be gone for twenty-four hours, and I'd hate you for it. I hated you showing up at the apartment the next day with that face of yours: two eyes like the tips of burned out cigarette butts, thin lips and yellow teeth, your hair all matted and greasy, a dirty smell hanging about you like you'd slept in a gutter somewhere. On nights like those, I'd fantasize about you being dead. That'd teach you. I'd picture you falling down dead drunk in the street and smashing your skull open on the sidewalk. A big pool of dark blood coming out of your mouth like a speech balloon. Otherwise, I'd just cry, sitting alone in our bedroom, despising myself. I'd dig my nails into my face until the skin was about to break.

Then there were the nights you'd come home from the bar or wherever, pacing the floor and talking to yourself about how unfair your life had been. Chain-smoking, knocking the ash onto the floor, spitting, ranting about your old man who split town after you were born and left you with some unwilling aunt who couldn't wait to be rid of you, either. You were so hard done by it was almost a joke. "You're embarrassing yourself," I said. "Everybody's got their own shit to deal with." But you hardly ever listened. Nights you did hear me, there would be a thrown ashtray, threats. Some nights you grabbed me by the throat. Ring any bells? But I felt bad for you. It was killing me, but I still felt so tenderly toward you. When you'd be out for the night, I'd smoke a joint, listening to the radio. I'd see these weird scenes in my head, sometimes, that seemed to come up out of nowhere. Like I'd made them up accidentally. Like a movie playing in my head. I saw us living in the country somewhere, a field of high grass spreading out before us down to the ocean, where the big black cliffs rose jagged and menacing from the waves. I saw the petals of wild roses in the gentle breeze hovering in the golden air above our heads. Rivers where you pulled trout from the current, the silver jetting shape of salmon. And sometimes, in this country paradise, I'd hallucinate killing you. Pulling a Lizzie Borden on you. Miles and miles from anywhere, I thought about taking a hatchet to your head. Putting your body in the garden where the apple tree grows, dew cold as January on the red skin. Then sometimes I'd see a girl in my mind's eye with an arm coming straight up out her cunt, like a picture from some fairy tale gone awry, and the hand at the end of the arm would be your hand. Your hand around this little girl's throat. Like what sometimes happened to me when you came home late and squeezed my windpipe until there were fireworks blotting out my vision. Because these are not the thoughts girls are supposed to have, I quit smoking dope, and haven't been tempted to go back to it since. But, to be honest, even now those sorts of dreams still happen. Remember how you'd always say you thought I was a little crazy? A little hysterical? I do. You told me they'd come to lock me away somewhere if it kept up.

And as I watched the apartment burn to the ground, I thought about these things. But you weren't there. I think you were at work. I don't even know what part of town you were

POWER

living in then. All I know is that you were still working at that café. The place we first met. Remember? I left origami cranes on the counter for you when you turned your back to make my coffee. I sure thought there was something special about you. They say if you make a thousand cranes while concentrating on something you want to happen, it'll come true for you. Did you know that? I must have gone to that café every day for a month. You had a girlfriend then, but I didn't care. And eventually, I saw you at the bar one night, and loosed my womanly charms on you. That's how you put it. You came home with me, and that was the beginning of our Love Affair. The way you said those words demonstrated that they were capitalized. You were the only one I ever chased like that, just so you know. I'm not the type of girl who goes moony-eyed over just anything.

And then the great exterior wall of the apartment came thundering down in a storm of ash and flame. Someone in the crowd shouted in triumph. Luke shivered in my arms. The whole edifice smoldered and blackened on the ground as I pulled the cat a little closer to my chest. My heart pounded and throbbed with blood and fear and love and rage. In the black ash and flankers swirling above our heads, I saw an image of your face. I kissed the white halo on Luke's head, black smoke encircling us.

I heard you moved to Spain. All you had ever wanted was to be a writer. I heard you wrote your novel. You worked on farms over there, traveled around. I heard the sun tanned you. Your hair got blonde. I heard you learned Spanish. You're living in a house now by the sea. You've taken up bird watching. I hear all kinds of things about you now, and it all seems like things have worked out terribly well for you. Someone told me they'd be surprised if you ever came back.

I don't think you should. That summer, they made the place where the apartment burned down into a parking lot. People park their cars right where our bed used to be. It's okay by me. Now, sitting here, writing this to you, I realize that unlike the cat, you were a fuck-load more trouble than you're worth.

AN APOLOGY

RAMONA DEARING

The first day of the trial will be the hardest. Gerard Lundrigan arrives at the courthouse exactly one hour early, at nine o'clock. Even then, the TV cameras are waiting, although they're not allowed inside the courtroom. He sits in that dark sanctuary, testing his chair. It will do. He's brought along the Graham Greene book he forgot to return to the library. But he can't read about the whiskey priest, not just yet. Gerard makes sure the buttons on his blue cardigan are done up right. He holds the book open, so it will look like he's doing something. Outside the tall windows is what looks to be the start of a March storm. He'd forgotten what it was like here. The wind is taking anything it can find. There's a good chance that, by noon, all of St. John's will be clamped in ice. Or it will be sunny, or raining, or snowing. You never knew about this place, he does remember that. He thinks about his pup back in Ontario, and how it likes to nose through the snow. It would like it here, especially rolling in landwash after chasing gulls.

AN APOLOGY

The jurors look nervous as they walk in. One woman giggles when she bumps into a chair on the way to the jury box, and her face stays red for a full hour. The other jurors' eyes swivel over the oak and mahogany scrollings, the ancient picture of the Queen, the thin, bunned judge in her red-sashed blue robe. A sheriff's officer walks around with one hand pressed to his ear piece, the other clamped at his hip to keep the keys on his belt from jingling. Two more sheriff's officers flank Gerard, tapping their fingers against their thighs. There can be trouble on the first day, apparently, scenes. The lawyers look edgy and clear their throats a lot. Gerard isn't sure how many spectators there are—he won't let himself look back. But there are eyes on him, of course—he can feel them. And he can see the jurors studying him. They've relaxed a bit, are sitting more deeply in their chairs. Not one of them looks like a leader. Not one of them looks to be well-studied. Only one man wears a tie. There's even a girl in jeans, chewing gum. They listen hard as the crown prosecutor outlines his case. During the preliminary inquiry, he'd been soft-spoken, methodical. Now he is playing to the jury, and there is insincerity and filth coming out his mouth. Absolute filth.

You're probably nervous, ladies and gentlemen of the jury. I know you are because I myself am nervous right now and I've been at this racket for a long time now. But there's no need to worry. All you have to do is sort through the facts, and I believe those facts are very clearly set out. You are the judge of the facts and as such, you will hear direct testimony that Brother Lundrigan beat little boys. Sodomized little boys. Ejaculated in their mouths as they gagged and struggled.

I know these are shocking things to say, sickening things to say. You probably wish you didn't have breakfast. All I can say is get used to it, because you're going to hear about it from eleven different men over the course of the next six weeks or so.

Most of the jurors suction their arms across their stomachs and keep them there all morning. Gerard sits very tall and looks straight ahead.

DEARING

The afternoon is better. The weather has settled somewhat. The first witness is called—the lead investigator from the Royal Newfoundland Constabulary. All he does is show a videotape of the orphanage, a long, long tape showing every room and closet and corridor and shed. The police shot the film before the wrecking ball knocked the place in on itself. There is the chapel, just as Gerard remembers it. The classrooms. The sleeping quarters. The gym. The old garden grounds. And so on, and on and on. All shot poorly, shakily, with bad lighting. But the courtroom has been darkened and, therefore, no one is staring at Gerard.

When the first complainant takes the stand, Gerard absorbs every word. He remembers the boy well. The one who'd wanted so badly to be on the gymnastics team but was disqualified because he failed math every year. He'd been a big boy then. Now, he has the look of a withered drunk. Ridiculous in a burgundy velvet jacket. Soft-spoken—the judge doesn't ask the man to speak up nearly enough. He didn't get that mumbling habit from his time at the orphanage. They'd taught pride there. Pride and decency and right-living.

The fellow goes on for hours about how terrible the orphanage was, how he and his younger brother would steal buns and hide them in the little barn for the times when they couldn't sleep for hunger. How they got in trouble just for sitting still, and worse beatings when they actually did anything bad. How Bro. Lundrigan was the worst one for the strap, especially with the boys in his dorm. How he wouldn't tolerate any illness and wouldn't let a boy go to the sickroom even if he'd thrown up all night. How Bro. Lundrigan would toss any boy who wet the bed into the swimming pool, no matter the time of year. How if he saw a boy crying for any reason, he'd rub soap in the child's eyes so he'd have something to screech about.

Gerard wants to speak. It's physically painful not to be able to respond, acid burning his gut. But since he won't be testi-

AN APOLOGY

fying for at least a month, he's started a notebook outlining every single point he disagrees with, numbering each in case it will help his lawyer.

23) No child ever went hungry in my care.

24) The strap had nothing to do with me. Blame the era, not the man. Do you think your disobedience made me happy—do you think I liked it?

25) I remember personally taking you to the sickroom on at least two occasions.

26) Re: soap—whatever are you talking about?

"Make him stop watching me," the first complainant says to the judge the fifth morning he's on the stand. The prosecutor has just started in on the buggery allegations. On the fire escape, one night. In the barn, many times. Many, many times. The witness's voice cracks. The judge orders a break.

117) The disgusting thing you allude to—where would I even have gotten the idea? What about my vows? Why would I do such a thing? You brought me here to watch your sickening tears and listen to you say these revolting things?

Gerard is thankful for his lawyer, who establishes in one efficient afternoon of cross-examination that the complainant has a long criminal record, including theft. He'd also attacked a man in a bar with a broken bottle. That's the kind of low-life he is. In and out of mental hospitals, with children spat out across northern Ontario like bits of gristle, and ex-wives lining up to get restraining orders.

The next witness is a real crowd-pleaser. Makes the jury smile as he remembers stringing chestnuts to play conkers. As he describes skinning his shins against the rough concrete of the swimming pool. The time Bro. Superior came in for breakfast one morning dressed like Charlie Chaplin and kept pretending to fall off his chair. What it was like riding the hay wagon into St. John's and seeing all those mesmerizing lights and the houses where you could look in the windows at the moms and dads and pops and nannies and little kids sitting right nice and sweet at the table.

He has them alright. Even the judge looks choked up. And then, less than half an hour later, he goes for a bull's-eye. His face is crazy red and he's dry-sobbing and beating one hand against the top of the witness box and pointing with the other: *That one, that one there. That bastard ruined me for everything. Your Honour, I'd as soon spit on him on his deathbed. That's a monster, that is. Not a man. Left me opened up and bleeding so's I couldn't shit for a week. Bite marks on my neck.*

The judge orders a break.

Gerard has begun to put together some theories. These men are forty-five, fifty. They're all into the booze or the drugs. They've all done time. He knows—it all came out at the preliminary hearing.

They've got something else in common: they've disappointed anyone who ever came into their lives. Including Gerard.

Their fathers were alcoholics or thieves or dead and their mothers were sluts or mad or dead. Now they're men looking to blame, to make someone accountable for their empty spots.

And who better than Gerard? They remember him making them sit on their bleeding hands—as was common in those times—and they want revenge, they want to make him sit on his own bleeding hands and get a taste of himself. They'd do that to a sixty-four-year-old because all they want is this one chance in their lives to give out orders and have someone obey.

So, okay, Gerard is sitting on his hands. They've got him where they want him. They wag their fingers like he used to in math class, and now it's him who can't talk back. It's so straightforward eye-for-an-eye that it's almost comic. Except what they really want is for him to fix their lives and that's something he never, ever could do.

A man is not a mother. A twenty-two-year old thinks he wants to get away from his slightly aristocratic parents. He thinks he wants to roll up his sleeves, get his hands dirty, serve.

AN APOLOGY

And so he does. And at first, God is everywhere. In the wind, in his ear, in the fellowship of the twenty-three-year-olds and the twenty-five-year-olds who also want nothing of society auctions and marriage and cigars. But there are fourteen boys in his charge. Two are just four years old, leggy babies with permanent ropes of snot hanging from their noses. Crying always for Mumma. The teen boys are revolting, with their acne and their smell and their trembling beds as they go at themselves in the dark. The middle ones are better, but still they hang off him, one on one arm, another on his back, another trying to get that one off. *Possums*, he'd called them, but he had to explain: no possums in Newfoundland.

Ripped off. Yes, they were. He always knew that. It wasn't easy for them. But it wasn't easy for him, either. Does anyone ever stop and think what it was like? Up at five-thirty for prayers with the other brothers. Getting the boys up at six and trying to get them to wash. Supervising breakfast. Teaching until four. Gymnastics coaching. Homework supervision. Somewhere in there making time to go over to the teachers' dorm and help out with the bed-bound ancient brothers. Then supervising his dorm, staying up all night, if necessary, with the croupy boys.

And those annual evaluations with the superior. Always getting on about the filth of the place, about how the boys needed to be pushed to do their chores properly. The lavatory like something out of India. How Bro. Superior wanted things pristine, the way they should be. And how the orphanage should be winning more trophies—how good it was for the boys to be the very best, to show them that adversity could be overcome.

One time, Gerard muttered under his breath *Yes, Bro., but what about my needs?* It had struck him as funny—by rights he'd prayed them all away hadn't he? That wasn't so long before he'd left. He remembers it was a Tuesday, and he'd walked back over to the main building and announced to all the boys at supper that there'd be no homework that night. They'd see *Gold Rush* instead and each boy could go to the canteen and pick out chips *and* a soda *and* a bar. All evening, he felt naughty and proud. But he tossed and turned in bed, worried he'd acted out of false pride.

After the third man takes the stand, Gerard decides he can't keep thinking about the past. What good does it do, dredging up these old details? He's got things happening in his life right now that need attention, and all because of this trial. His lawyer has told him to keep taking notes. But everything that is being said has already been said twice before and presumably will go around nine more times. The jurors are starting to look bored. They get sent out of the courtroom a lot while the lawyers argue whether certain lines of questioning should be allowed. Gerard has heard the sheriff's officers say the women are knitting up a storm during the time they wait downstairs in the jury room and that one of them brought in this cappuccino machine they're all going mad for.

The lawyers have settled into a steadiness, a matter-of-factness. It has been seven weeks now. They joke about being here for another three months.

Here, I am just a bit taller than the door latch—I can feel it digging in back of my head—and here he is picking me up by my ears and telling me to clamp it or everything is going to hurt more.

More and more, all Gerard can think of is the pup and how it's doing. He remembers the little squeaky sound it makes when it yawns. He doesn't know why he got it with the trial coming up, but he did. He wasn't going to, but then the trial was postponed for the second time, some conflict with the judge's schedule. He just saw the pup—in a pet store, of all places—and took it home.

He'd felt like a new mother. Every sound led back to the pup. He was in the library one day when he was sure he could hear Brigus keening. Gerard had stood there waiting for claws to scrape white lines on his shins. But, of course, the dog wasn't there. The sound must have been a pencil sharpener or some such thing.

AN APOLOGY

Walking home the long way, the pretty way—along the Avon and its low-waisted willows, past Tom Patterson Island, past the Stratford Festival Theatre, past the squirrels—another squeal from Brigus, except really it came from a gull. And the next false alarm was a scream of brakes from a bus.

When he'd returned home to the pup, a copy of *The Power and the Glory* warming his armpit, there was only the sound of his keys hitting the table and a metronome of tail hitting the sides of the crate. Thump thump thump thump, etc.

I never told no one until my lady put it on the line. She said, "Look, my honey, you've got something eating you all these years and it's eating me too and I'm falling apart and I don't even know why."

He wonders how the house-sitter is making out. He calls her a couple of times a week and she says everything's fine, but he wonders if that's really the case. It bothers him, having someone in his house. But what can he do? The pup can't be abandoned.

He'd put an ad in the paper for a caretaker. The girl answered and so did some older women and a boy maybe twenty-one. He interviewed the boy and liked him best, but decided against him on the basis of the trouble factor with boys. The women talked too much. The girl was quiet. He had her move in the week before he left just to make sure he could trust her. She didn't spend any time on the phone, which surprised him. She washed her dishes as soon as she finished eating. She spent all her time with the pup, mostly outside.

He'd told her he didn't know how long he'd be gone on business. Depended how the deal went. Not too long, he didn't think.

"You still working?" It was the only question she ever asked him. He'd nodded. At night, he could hear her drag the nightstand up against her door. She kept the pup in with her.

I said, "Lord Jesus, take me out of this." And then I tried with the razor. I really wanted it. I would picture Bro. Lundrigan walking past my casket getting all shaky.

DEARING

Okay, he's not a saint. There are times he's picked Brigus up by the gruff and shook him and whacked him, once even in front of the girl. You can only trip down the stairs so many times with forty-eight ounces of stupidity skinning your heel. You can only pick up gummed toilet paper so many times off the living room floor, say goodbye to so many boots and tea towels. Gerard had taken to reading a book on dog training by some monks who raise and sell drug-sniffing German Shepherds at their monastery in New York State. He'd read it at four-thirty in the morning, wide awake after taking the dog outside for its first shit of the day. While Gerard read, Brigus would curl tight, a potato bug on the floor next to the bedframe. The monks say to never give in to exasperation. Stay in control. *To stop biting, give the snout a firm but harmless shake. Expect a yelp of surprise. Hold the palm flat and ask for a lick instead. Praise your pup.* Sometimes Gerard has grabbed the pup's snout just to make it cry out.

Brigus never seems to bite the girl. She's to dust and vacuum and scrub every week. No visitors. She'll be needing to keep the lawn cut and the garden tidy. "You understand everything I'm paying you to do?" he'd said. She'd nodded. It was his parents' house, he told her, and needed to be treated with that kind of respect. She'd nodded again. The pup was to be her first priority, though. Another nod, this time with a slight smile attached.

He wonders if she's having parties. If there are people fornicating in his house right now. In his parents' old bed. He decides to call again at the lunch break.

No answer, for the fourth day in a row.

The fifth complainant knocks the hell out of him. Gerard has no idea who he is. He knows he didn't recognize the name, but he thought when he saw the fellow it would all click. The man hadn't made it to the prelim, and now that Gerard is finally looking right at him, he can't place him at all.

At lunch he says to his lawyer, "How could I not know one of the children?"

AN APOLOGY

His lawyer looks tired. "What's to remember when you're dealing with a liar?"

The records point to Gerard teaching the man for three years—he apparently failed Grade Seven math. He's convinced the man must have had another name back then. How could Gerard forget one of the boys?

The lack of giving in the dog really surprised him. He wishes he could talk to the New York State monks about that. They'd know what he means. It sits there insisting on being noticed, forever complaining. Something the orphans never would have dared. Fat Brigus, ears flopping back and forth as he pisses on the bathmat, wants chicken, wrestling matches, lap naps, and cheese.

Surely the dog will still know him when he gets back?

He remembers the eleventh complainant in great detail. A sweet boy he was, needy, but still sweet. Had these fat ringlets and a long skinny frame. Gerard's favourite possum, always leaning in, content. *Look what I got you, Brother.* And in his fist a wet stone, one side glowing an ashy red if the light hit it right. Gerard would pick him up and hold him tight.

He's grey now and has his hair clipped. Still thin, though. He would have loved Brigus, that boy, would have petted him bald. *If you pinches the pads on their feet they won't jump up no more, isn't that right? You gots to give them a big squirt of a squeeze whenever they does that. Can I touch his tail, Brother? I mean, may I, Bro.?*

The mother of the eleventh man gets herself in the paper. Apparently, she's been in the public gallery through the whole trial. She waits until her boy's finished testifying. He has been crying softly for the last hour or so on the stand. But the mother doesn't go to her son. No, as soon as the judge leaves the courtroom, she walks up behind Gerard and tugs on the elbow of his cardigan and explains who she is.

No one else has spoken to him, aside from his lawyer. The reporters look down when he walks past them. The sheriff's officers never speak directly to him. "Does Mr. Lundrigan want some water?" they'll ask his lawyer. The clerks don't look at him. Even in corner stores, if he's buying a paper or some chocolate, no one looks right at him. Sometimes the cashier won't hold her hand out to take the money, forcing him to leave it on the counter and forget about the change.

But the mother smiles. "I've forgiven you," she says.

Gerard's lawyer moves closer.

"I've thought about it and you're going to do your time and you should get at least one more little chance, you know. I mean, who in frig am I to rebuke you? I mean, I'm the one who handed over my boy, right?"

The spectators who are getting ready to put on their coats are like hares, all ears and eyes.

The woman's voice is getting louder, too. "I kept saying he's just a man, same as any other. Just a man. That's how I'm going to look at you, anyway. Others might not, but I'm going to. For me, you know. For myself. Important, you know?"

Gerard turns from her, reaches for his coat.

She comes around on the other side, so that she's still facing him. The reporters are there now, too, holding out microphones. "I mean, nothing can give back my Sean what you took, so why should we keep after you, really? I mean, jail, yes. Go to jail for a while, you definitely should do that. But hatred, that's no good."

"Okay, okay," the sheriff's officers say. "This courtroom's closed for the day." They have their hands on her elbows and are edging her back, gently.

She says, "Do you have a message I could bring to the boys for you?"

He puts his arms across his chest and hates himself for doing it.

"Len Stamps, Red Matthews, Tom Walsh. You remember them all, right? Plus my Sean, of course."

AN APOLOGY

The officers are getting her closer to the door. She's pushing against them.

"Donnie Hawko. Bill Wheaton, John Cooke, Vince Rutherford. You heard them. You heard what they said."

The reporters are following her, trying to ask her questions. But she ignores them.

"Say you're sorry," she yells. "Say 'I apologize.' Just say that. You'll feel better."

The next afternoon, Gerard is on the stand. The only witness for the defense. Some of the other Brothers wouldn't take the stand at their trials. But the juries didn't like that, apparently. Besides, Gerard doesn't mind talking. There's no way he can keep sitting on his hands.

The jury will see the authority he carries, the calm. The jury will remember the complainants and their mental illnesses, their criminal records. The roughness about them.

Except, when he first gets on the stand, he feels like he might pass out. Everywhere he looks, he sees set faces.

He imagines the girl bringing Brigus here, coming in through the spectators' door and letting him off the lead at the back of the courtroom, a much bigger Brigus running at full hurl to cover Gerard with licks. He sees everyone smiling: the judge, the jury, the audience, himself.

After that, he gets his confidence back. *We wanted those boys to have a chance in the world. We pushed them. We made it clear everything was going to be hard for them. We didn't believe in pretending they weren't orphans.*

On the Sunday before cross-examination is to start, the girl answers the phone. She tells him she's seen his picture in the paper. She says she'll take care of the dog no matter what but she doesn't know if she can stay in the house because it is too sickening. She is thinking about going home to her parents and taking Brigus with her. "No," Gerard says. "You have to stay." If she leaves, she could steal everything on her way out. She could write things on the walls. She could set the house on fire. She could take Brigus and never give him back.

"Who exactly are you to be setting the rules?" she says, and he understands then her quietness is not as peaceful as he'd thought.

All he can say is, "Please, it's not whatever you're thinking." And offer extra money.

The crown attorney mocks him. "You mean, you taught this man for three years but can't remember him? Therefore, if you can't remember him, we're to conclude you're innocent? Okay, let's look at that. Let's say you couldn't remember whether you'd filed your income taxes for last year. Let's say it turns out you didn't. Does that mean, in the eyes of Revenue Canada, that you're off the hook, Mr. Lundrigan?"

Gerard can only repeat what he's already said several times: "I know the records indicate that man was in my classroom three years running, but I also know I'd never laid eyes on him before this trial started, so how could I have done these terrible things as he claims?"

The jury finds that amusing. The judge calls a break.

There's another bad moment on what turns out to be Gerard's last day of cross-examination. It involves the allegations of the last complainant, Sean.

"Did you ever, Mr. Lundrigan, slip your tongue into his mouth as alleged?"

"No. But perhaps once when I kissed him there might have been an accident."

"You kissed the boy?"

"Yes, many times. Like a mother."

"On the lips?"

"Yes, sir. Like a mother would."

"Did you kiss the other boys?"

"No, sir."

AN APOLOGY

"Why not?"

"He was special, very dear to me, innocent. He needed affection."

"So you kissed him on the lips?"

"I've already answered that."

"Like a mother?"

"Like a mother."

"Did you ever insert your penis into his mouth?"

"Of course not."

"Even by accident?"

Gerard's lawyer objects, and the judge agrees. She calls an early lunch break.

Gerard's lawyer says he can't eat with him today—he has to run to the dentist. A weak lie, since normally they'd still be in session.

Gerard sees Sean's mother putting on her coat in the last row of benches in the public gallery. He wouldn't let himself look over that way when he was on the stand. Now, she won't look at him.

The judge gives her charge to the jury. It takes two days for her to finish. Gerard spends the time working on an apology to the boys, but nothing comes out right.

I have no malice towards you. You came to us robbed. We were only boys ourselves, you forget that.

I'm sorry you made me come here.

I'm sorry you've made such a fuss.

I'm sorry you want my blood.

To think he wiped their asses.

A pity his lawyer would never let him send a letter. It might help them.

The jury is out. Gerard's lawyer gives him a cell phone and tells him to stay within a ten-minute radius of the courtroom. The lawyer says not to fret if the deliberations take several days—the longer, the better. "I'd hang out with you," the lawyer says, "but I'm just snow-balled with work at the office."

At first, Gerard stays in the little apartment he's rented. He knew the wait was going to be bad, but not this bad. If he lies on the bed, the ceiling comes down to a point just above his nose. The more he paces, the more he sees himself in the mirrors that are all over the room. If he looks out the window, he feels lonely.

The harbour is quiet. The *Astron* is in, and a fisheries patrol vessel. Some longliners. It is sunny, and even better, it's windy. Somehow, the gusts comfort him. It's a clean wind here, a wind that leaves the good in you.

It licks at him as he starts winding up the road to Signal Hill. Maybe no one will recognize him with his ear flaps down. Not that he's hiding—it's the kind of cold that makes your ear drums ache.

The flags at Cabot Tower flap like tents in a blizzard. The few people walking around up here actually nod at him. It's a community of sorts, brought on by the elements.

He looks down at Chain Rock. He could aim for it. There's no way he could even come close. But he could tell himself that's what he was doing. The wind would rub him against a rock face on the way down. If he waits until he's a bit colder he probably wouldn't feel a thing.

He remembers his last day with the dog. Not even that went right. He'd only meant to nudge Brigus toward the door with his foot but, for some reason, he'd kicked the pup good and hard. He'd spent forever trying to get it out from under the couch. In the end, Gerard set up a semi-circle of cheese cubes, like stepping stones to the centre of the living room.

Outside, they'd passed through the art gallery grounds to get down to the river. Brigus barreled through the steel sculpture that looks like an oversized napkin holder and then spun around, checking to make sure he could still see Gerard. When they got over the railroad tracks and down the hill, the

AN APOLOGY

dog hacked after studiously and sombrely licking a mound of dirt. Gerard had felt like whipping himself. "I'm no good for you," he'd said, and walked away, fast. But no matter where he stepped, he could hear the pup rushing the grass right behind.

What you do and what you mean. Two entirely different things. Gerard never meant anyone any trouble.

He does mean to push off right now, but he can't do it.

He heads down the footpath to the Interpretation Centre, where there are payphones—he's not allowed to tie up the cell phone. Gerard calls his house and, miraculously, she picks up.

"You're still there?" he says.

"I need the money, okay?"

"That's fine," he says, "I'm happy."

No response.

Gerard tries again. "He's your dog, okay? You take him. If you go."

The wind makes him cry on the way back down the hill. It keeps grinding bits of dirt right in there. He's hurrying because he's just now understanding it's not going to take the jury long.

There's so much wind, he wonders whether he'll even hear the phone if it rings in his pocket.

But he does. He's surprised how relieved he feels.

ABOUT THE AUTHORS

KATHLEEN WINTER is the author of the short fiction collection, *boYs* (Biblioasis), winner of the Winterset and Metcalf-Rooke awards. Her novel, *Annabel* (House of Anansi), is scheduled for spring 2010.

GERARD COLLINS is a St. John's writer who has worn many disguises while conspiring to be a full-time writer. He has published short stories in *Storyteller*, *Zeugma* and *TickleAce* and won a handful of writing prizes, including the Percy Janes First Novel Award. Having finished a doctorate on ghosts in literature, he is now working on a gothic novel and haunting the downtown coffee shops.

ELIZABETH BLANCHARD lives in Dieppe, New Brunswick. Her work has appeared in a number of literary journals including *Dalhousie Review*, *Lichen Arts & Letters Preview*, *Windsor Review* and *Room of One's Own*. In 2007, she won the Writers' Federation of New Brunswick Literary Competition, and she has recently been awarded a Creation Grant by the New Brunswick Arts Board.

LESLIE VRYENHOEK is a writer, editor and communications consultant whose poetry, fiction and non-fiction have appeared in magazines and journals across Canada and internationally. Her work has won the Eden Mills Literary Festival competition, the Cahoots Fiction contest and the Dalton Camp Award, and placed in the Sheldon Currie Fiction Contest (*The Antigonish Review*) and *This Magazine's* Great Canadian Literary Hunt (poetry). Her debut book of short stories, *Scrabble Lessons*, will be published in fall 2009 by Oolichan Books. She lives in St. John's.

MICHELLE BUTLER HALLETT is the author of the novel *Double-blind* and *The shadow side of grace*, a collection of short fiction, both published by Killick Press. Butler Hallett lives in St. John's with her husband and two daughters.

STEVE VERNON is a Maritime writer and storyteller who has been spinning his own brand of dark-edged storytelling for many years. His first three collections of ghost stories—*Haunted Harbours*, *Wicked Woods* and *Halifax Haunts* are available from Nimbus Publishing. Steve's brand new children's picture book *Maritime Monsters: A Field Guide* is being released in the fall of 2009. Steve is currently working on several YA novels and his next ghost story collection.

LEE D. THOMPSON was born and raised in Moncton, New Brunswick. His short fiction has appeared in literary journals across Canada and in the anthologies *Victory Meat: New Fiction from Atlantic Canada*, *New Brunswick Short Stories*, and *The Vagrant Revue of New Fiction*. His book *S. a novel in [xxx] dreams* was published by Broken Jaw Press in 2007. Editor of the fiction journal *Galleon*, he has twice been awarded Creation Grants from ARTSNB and a Creation Grant from the Canada Council for the Arts. He is currently executive director of the Writers' Federation of New Brunswick.

KEITH COLLIER grew up on Newfoundland's South Coast and attended Memorial University. He now works as a writer and researcher in St. John's and has published articles in a number of magazines and newspapers, including *The Independent* and *The Newfoundland Quarterly*.

JOANNE SOPER-COOK was born in outport Newfoundland. She is the author of six critically acclaimed novels—most recently *A Cold-Blooded Scoundrel*—and a book of short fiction, *The Opium Lady*. Her writings have been widely anthologized and have been published via radio, stage and print media. She designed, developed, and currently teaches "Write Naturally," an online, self-directed creativity learning method. She lives in St. John's with her husband of twenty years, Paul Cook, and their two "fur kids" Lola and Shep.

MICHAEL CRUMMEY is the author of three books of poetry, *Arguments with Gravity*, winner of the Writer's Alliance of Newfoundland and Labrador Book Award for Poetry, *Hard Light* and, most recently, *Salvage*. He has also published a book of short stories, *Flesh & Blood*; three acclaimed, bestselling novels, *River Thieves*, *The Wreckage* and *Galore*; and collaborated with photographer Greg Locke on *Newfoundland: Journey into a Lost Nation*. He lives in St. John's, Newfoundland.

SARA TILLEY'S writing spans the genres of playwriting, prose and poetry. She has written, co-written or co-created over ten plays to date, all of which have received professional production. *Skin Room*, her first novel (Pedlar Press, 2008), won both the 2004 Newfoundland and Labrador Percy Janes First Novel Award and the inaugural Fresh Fish Award for Emerging Writers in 2006. *Skin Room* is shortlisted for the Winterset Award and the Thomas Raddall Atlantic Fiction Prize.

DON ROY is a graduate of St. Francis Xavier University with a degree in English. He is at the final revisions of his first novel and writes short stories as a diversion. In the past two years, he has completed The Wired Studio at The Banff Center, been awarded a creation grant to finish his novel by the Nova Scotia Department of Tourism, Culture and Heritage and is currently participating in a mentorship sponsored by The Writers Federation of Nova Scotia. Don lives in Antigonish, Nova Scotia with his three teenage children.

CRAIG FRANCIS POWER is a visual artist and writer from St. John's. His novel *Blood Relatives*, won the Writers Alliance of Newfoundland and Labrador's 2007 Fresh Fish Award and the 2008 Percy Janes First Novel Award. It is forthcoming from Pedlar Press in the fall of 2010.

RAMONA DEARING lives in St. John's, Newfoundland. Her poems and short stories have appeared in *The Malahat Review*, *Grain* and *Prairie Fire*, as well as in *Oberon's Best Canadian Stories and Coming Attractions*. She is a member of the writing collective The Burning Rock. She works for CBC Radio.

ABOUT THE EDITOR

MIKE HEFFERNAN was born and raised in St. John's, Newfoundland. He is the author of *Rig: An Oral History of the Ocean Ranger Disaster*, which is being adapted for the stage. His most recent work has appeared in *The Newfoundland Quarterly*, *Our Times* and *Riddle Fence* and performed on CBC Radio. He is currently working on *The Other Side of Midnight: Taxi Cab Stories*.

ABOUT THE ILLUSTRATOR

DARREN WHALEN was formally trained as a visual artist at Sir Wilfred Grenfell College in Corner Brook, Newfoundland. After graduating in 2005 he moved back to his hometown of St. John's where he currently resides.

His paintings consist mostly of large scale figurative works. The art work for *Hard Ol' Spot* is the result of his passion for illustration, background in publishing, and a desire to create something uniquely Atlantic Canadian.

ACKNOWLEDGEMENTS

When I started this book, *TickleAce* hadn't published in over a decade and there was no *Riddle Fence*. Newfoundland was bursting at the seams with literary talent but there was nowhere in the province for our emerging fiction writers to further develop their skills or for our established professionals to share new work. I tried to remedy that, in some small way.

The fourteen stories of *Hard Ol' Spot: An Anthology of Atlantic Canadian Fiction* are comfortable tackling the uncomfortable. They have a social conscience. There is a rough geography and a dark urban landscape. There are only so many writers around willing to put these kinds of ideas to paper, requiring me to cast a wide editorial net. But all fourteen stories are uniquely East Coast. Without the authors' trust and kind patience, this book would not exist.

The illustrator and I have been friends for a long time, and we've always had it in mind to collaborate on at least one major project. I was lucky to have Darren's unwavering dedication and enthusiasm. This book is an exhibition of his exceptional talents.

For loving me, no matter what: Lesley and Anja.

Donna Francis and Creative Book Publishing, who rescued this book from the ashes.

A number of organizations made this book a possibility: Newfoundland and Labrador Arts Council, Writers' Alliance of Newfoundland and Labrador, Writers' Federation of New Brunswick, Writer's Federation of Nova Scotia, Prince Edward Island Writers' Guild, Eastern Edge Gallery, Pick Me Up Artist Collective and CBC.